BITTER REVENGE

TERESA WOODWORTH

Enjoy!

Teresa

To my Dad, Roy E. Brown, Jr. Although you have been gone twelve years, your stories and jokes continue on through your kids.

PROLOGUE

H is six-foot frame was quiet and still. His elbows rested on his knees and his lips were pressed against his steepled fingers.

Danger radiated below the surface.

Mark Franklin had waited a long time for this moment and in less than an hour he would be out of this hellhole.

His face was strong and well defined, his aristocratic heritage reflected in the bone structure. The deep-set eyes and square jaw had made many women's, as well as men's, heads turn. He had a power and confidence that could not be ignored. A power that inspired awe and commanded everyone's attention as soon as he stepped into a room.

Mark sat on the edge of the bed, his dark blue eyes focused on the spot where the wall met the floor. .

He glanced around the small cell that held only a bed and toilet. The so-called bed was nothing more than a beat-up, worn-down mattress that hadn't once provided him a good night's sleep. The cell had been a constant reminder of the luxury he no longer possessed. Instead of expensive artwork in a warm, inviting room where he could entertain clients, he had stared at cold, gray cement walls for almost three years.

He had always been driven and escaping from prison was one more hurdle he would jump. So he continued to wait patiently.

His drive and his patience were going to help him escape this rat hole.

For years, his name had been famously linked with the financial district. He had been a well-respected financial advisor/stockbroker and was sought after by anyone and everyone who had a substantial amount of money.

The empathy and understanding he projected had made his clients feel comfortable. Comfortable enough to give him their complete trust along with their money. They believed he honestly had their best interests in mind. This, along with his proficiency, had helped him in his pursuit of fortune.

He had planned it all meticulously. His goals had been to achieve the respect of the financial industry, gain financial independence, and marry and have kids. He had gained respectability as quickly as he made money. His clients adored him. But on his way to independence, his carefully laid plans had been knocked out from under him. And that was her fault.

Mark stood and started pacing the limited space. Although he controlled most of his emotions without difficulty, the mere thought of his ex-fiancée, Sandra Johnson, brought on a vicious rage that bubbled beneath his skin.

She was the reason he was behind bars. Little did she know she was the driving force behind his prison escape. He smiled and the tension slowly left his body.

Walking to his cell door, Mark wrapped his long fingers around the bars of the small window and listened for his freedom. He heard the familiar sounds of the guard making the final rounds as he paused and made small talk with a number of the inmates. As the guard moved from cell to cell, he whistled, the soft fall of his footsteps noticeable on the concrete flooring. Mark could tell he was only a few minutes away. His plan was ready to put into action. He returned to his bed and sat, anticipating his freedom.

Sandra had often commented that she was drawn to him because of his eyes. His eyes were what had captivated her and now his eyes would be the last things she would see.

Chapter 1

This had to be a joke. But Sandra didn't think any part of what the two men in front of her were saying was funny. She looked out at the busy street from a window of the small gym she owned and then closed her eyes and stretched her neck from side to side. Sandra opened one eye to find the two men, who had identified themselves as U.S. Marshals, still standing in front of her waiting for a response. She slightly shook her head hoping clarification, or at least sanity, would prevail. Instead, the movement only caused loose strands of hair to fall across her eyes. She brushed them away.

Perhaps the men in front of her were part of a dream. She'd had stranger dreams. The scene certainly had attributes of a dream.

One of the men was over six feet tall, dark and certainly would turn a woman's head. She guessed his age to be in the mid-thirties.

He was a little uptight for her taste. There wasn't a wrinkle to be found on his suit, his tie was straight, and for all she knew, glued into place so even a strong wind wouldn't move it. His hair was neat and precise. She wondered what he would do if she reached up and mussed his hair. Would he shoot her on the spot or simply brush his hair back into place?

The brown eyes studying her were intense. The slightly crooked nose could have been broken from football while the scar near his right eyebrow made her think "street fight." Broad shoulders filled out his suit jacket and his leanness was that of a runner. There was nothing warm and fuzzy about him. Could he be allergic to smiling?

The second man was young. Lanky with a boyish appearance, he made Sandra wonder how long he had been out of high school. His dark suit was a little too big and not close to the quality of Mr. Tall, Dark and Silent's, suggesting he may have grabbed the attire from a basement discount store. For the life of her, she couldn't understand why he kept smiling. With big, pale blue eyes and dark brown hair falling across his forehead, he seemed eager as a puppy waiting for his master to tell him to fetch.

Sandra decided she must have misunderstood.

"I'm sorry, I must not have heard you correctly." She brushed another piece of hair from her face. "Could you please explain to me again why you are here?"

"We're here to protect you, Miss Johnson." This statement came from the boy-man. He was grinning from ear-to-ear, obviously pleased with his answer.

"Because?" Sandra thought she was going to have to pull the explanation out of them one word at a time. The one grinning did nothing to alleviate her mounting fears, but glancing at Mr. Tall, Dark and Silent didn't help those fears, either.

"Ma'am, is there a place where we can talk privately?"

Mr. Tall and Dark finally spoke again in that deep voice. He nodded his head in the direction of Sandra's one client. Sandra glanced at Judy Travis and noted she had started her second round of circuit training.

"Before we do that," Sandra replied, "let's start at the beginning with introductions again and the appropriate identifications."

"Certainly, Ma'am." Mr. Tall and Dark's lips barely moved.

"Please don't call me "Ma'am." You can call me Ms. Johnson."

"Yes, Ms. Johnson."

The way he pronounced her name made Sandra think of lemons. Mr. Tall and Dark appeared to want to be anywhere, but standing in front of her. She could only assume he had drawn the short stick for this assignment.

"My name is Trey Walker and my partner here is Danny Logan. We are U.S. Marshals on assignment to protect you."

As if on cue, both men flipped out their badges in her direction and just as quickly closed them before slipping them back into their jackets.

"Okay, now this time slower with the badges. I want to touch them and read them. You know, for authenticity."

Sandra noted her sarcasm was not lost on Walker. His eyes changed a fraction. A glimmer of acknowledgement maybe? Sandra mentally gave herself a point for prompting a reaction from him. His puppy dog sidekick was an open book, however, and he momentarily lost a little of the happiness in his smile.

"Oh, Ms. Johnson, our apologies. Of course you can look at them." Logan practically fell all over himself trying to retrieve the badge from his pocket. He caught the metal shield on every corner of his suit pocket before yanking so hard that the badge went flying across the room. He scrambled after it as if chasing a tossed ball.

Sandra covered her mouth. The chaos was like watching Laurel and Hardy without Hardy. Even Judy stopped in the middle of her lunges to watch. The lines in Walker's brow had deepened as he watched Logan retrieve his badge. If she hadn't been watching closely, she would have missed the slight shake of his head and the whispered sigh that escaped.

Sandra noted that Walker's face briefly revealed his lack of tolerance for Logan. What an unhappy man. Did he have any social skills? Or did Walker simply put up walls?

Where Logan had trouble pulling his badge free from his pocket, Walker was smoothed and practiced. He continued to watch Logan only refocusing his attention on her when she took the badge from him. Sandra handed the badge back, thanking him. A returned, "you're welcome" was not forthcoming.

He must be very lonely, she thought. Perhaps he didn't have any family. There's no way he had a girlfriend unless she was as uptight as he appeared. Of course, that could explain his behavior. No girlfriend, no sex. Sex always improved a person's outlook on life.

Logan, still the eager puppy, passed his badge to Sandra and she dutifully examined the identification.

Walker was still staring at her, the lack of patience evident on his face. He must have mastered the expression over time. Although, perhaps not. Maybe disgust came naturally to him. He was wound tight and she would venture to guess he was a "strictly by the book" kind of guy.

Sandra motioned for them to follow her. "We'll have more privacy back here. Judy, be sure and let me know if you need help. I'll just be a few minutes."

Although she had addressed her client like she would have any other day, Sandra knew better. Today wasn't any other day. After all, the Marshals had mentioned her ex-fiancée when they first arrived and certainly no good could come after that disclosure.

———

T REY W ALKER WATCHED Sandra walked around her desk. She was a little taller than the average woman and had a "don't-screw-with-me" confidence. But then, she wouldn't have been successful in her business if she didn't. Her flashing green eyes offset her dark red hair. Red hair was a trait associated with a quick temper. There were exceptions, of course, but Trey would bet she wasn't one of them.

His physical response to her had taken him by surprise. His dating life had been on the slow side as of late. Perhaps the response was a reminder to take time to play. His assignments had been especially exhausting lately barely leaving time for checking in with his family. He smirked, knowing his mother would have jumped all over the idea. Not that he planned on sharing that information with her anytime soon. Or ever. Her mission in life was to see him happily married with at least two and half kids and a house with a white picket fence.

Refocusing on Sandra Johnson, he wondered what about her was attractive to him. She was pretty, confidant, and in good shape, but over the years he had met lots of women who had those qualities.

After reading her file that she owned a gym, he realized he had been expecting more of a body-builder type.

Sandra Johnson wasn't even close to the muscle-bound, almost manly weightlifters you saw on television. She had curves in all the right places and appeared younger than her thirty-three years. Perhaps what he was expecting, hard-core, massive muscles, and the feminine beauty he was presented upon meeting her was the reason he was responding like any warm-blooded male. She probably drove the men in town wild. Unless, of course, there was one particular man in her life. Mentally he flipped through her file. No, there hadn't been anything regarding a significant other.

He waited until she was seated before he sat down. Or at

least tried. Instead he bumped into a grinning Logan who was sitting where Trey had intended. When Logan finally clued in that Trey expected to sit in the chair he occupied, his face turned a little red. Logan stood and circled around to the other chair.

One minute Logan was upright and the next he was sprawled on the floor. At least he had managed to catch himself before making face-to-floor contact.

This, thought Trey Walker, was the trouble with the department's new policy of getting support staff out in the field. And, they had purposely given him a wet-behind-the-ears computer geek. After spending only a half a day with him, Trey knew time with him was going to take twice as much of his energy to do this assignment. He would inevitably be picking up pieces Logan dropped. His co-workers must be having a good laugh back at the office. Someone would pay. When he returned to the office, Trey would find out who had assigned him Logan and he would make sure the favor was returned.

Trey closed his eyes and slowly counted to ten.

When he opened them, Sandra was leaning over her desk. "Mr. Logan, are you all right?"

Logan jumped up and tugged at his suit, smoothing things back into place. "Yes, Ms. Johnson, I'm fine." He grinned at her, not at all embarrassed. "It must be these new shoes."

New shoes, my ass.

Trey rubbed his eyes, noting a headache waiting in the wings. Logan was a tall, gangly man who was still trapped in teenage awkwardness with thin arms and legs that seemed to go opposite directions every time he moved. Logan reminded him of a puppet on strings. Trey might have thought someone was pulling a clever trick on him if it wasn't for the fact that Logan talked without assistance.

Apparently feeling put together, Logan managed to settle into the chair with an apologetic grin plastered on his face.

Sandra slowly sank back into her chair and abruptly closed her mouth. She was obviously puzzled, not only by what had happened, but also by the young man. He knew exactly how she felt.

"Ms. Johnson, you're familiar with Mark Franklin?"

"Geez, Boss, of course she is." Logan's silly grin was back and he rolled his eyes at Sandra as if they were in on a joke. "He used to be her fiancée." He clicked his tongue and shook his head.

Trey sent a look to silence him, that, for once he read and obeyed.

Sandra appeared to feel sorry for Logan, because when she turned her attention back to Trey, her sympathy had been replaced with an expression of disgust. Now he remembered why he had taken a leave of absence from dating. If she only knew how far Trey's patience had been pushed after being with Logan for the last—was it only four hours? — she might be more concerned about Trey's well being.

"As your side-kick pointed out, Mr. Walker, he used to be my fiancée."

She folded her arms across her chest and leaned back in her chair. In his line of work, reading body language was Trey's business. Her eyes were cautious. The woman in front of him was, no doubt, fighting her instincts not to run at the mere mention of

Mark Franklin. His name was probably enough to send tidal waves of shock and bad memories coursing through her. The rapid pulse at the base of her neck and the flush spreading along her chest and neck told the story. She wouldn't be good at poker.

"So what does he have to do with your visit?"

She unfolded her arms, leaned forward and repositioned her arms on the desk, clasping her hands together. She rubbed her right thumb back and forth over her left hand.

"You haven't heard." It was a simple statement.

"Heard what, Mr. Walker?"

"Mark Franklin escaped from prison last night."

Sandra sucked in a breath and jerked to a sitting position, visibly paling. For a second, Trey felt sorry for Sandra Johnson. The report on Mark Franklin had been one of a man whose ego was out of whack. He had seen the pictures of Sandra after Franklin had tried running her over. Her angels must have worked overtime that day, for only a miracle could explain why she was still alive. Although she bore no visible scars, the internal scars would never fully go away. Trey had been on too many cases not to know. Not to have seen families dealing with horrific losses and how they all had to find a new normal.

"Prisons are to keep bad people locked up. Mark Franklin is a bad person. What the hell are prisons for if you can't keep the prisoners inside?"

Ignoring her sarcasm and rising temper, he continued, "As representatives of the U.S. Marshal Service, we are here to protect you. Mark Franklin very publicly threatened to come after you when he was released from prison. We have reason to believe he will do exactly as he said."

Trey wasn't sure what kind of reaction he was expecting from her. Having done this for years, though, he knew inside she was scared to death. Her bravado was only a wall to hide behind. Under the stress of such news, the wall was understandable. But he knew, too, the wall would crumble and she would once again feel vulnerable. Fleetingly he wondered who would help her pick up those pieces. Family? A new boyfriend?

Sandra pushed to a standing position and Trey and Logan followed suit. Her body's response made it obvious she was not warming to the idea that they were there to safeguard her.

"Mr. Walker, in view of how our prison system seems to operate, I don't see how having you here to *protect* me is a guarantee that Mark won't contact me. And if the agency sent their best," Sandra waved her hand towards Logan, "then forgive me for not jumping on the bandwagon. I have a better chance of Mr. Logan running into me and knocking me in front of a bus. I'd rather take my chances with Mark." Sandra made eye contact with Logan. "No offense."

"None taken, Ms. Johnson." Logan continued to look like an eager puppy.

Although Sandra didn't seem hysterical about the prospect of her former fiancée hunting her down, the change in her speech pattern and the slight shake in her hands were not lost on Trey. Thankfully her color was coming back.

"I know having Franklin break out of prison doesn't bode well, Ms. Johnson. However, I *guarantee* I will not let any harm come to you." As if to rectify the Logan situation, he added, "Regardless of who is assigned to me."

He watched her digest his comment. Satisfied she had and that she would be willing to continue their conversation, he indicated for her to sit again. After a moment's hesitation, she complied.

"We understand this will be difficult, but I promise you that this situation can be resolved quickly and efficiently."

"Efficient for whom, Mr. Walker? As I see it, you two being here wouldn't have been necessary if Mark hadn't escaped from prison to begin with, don't you think?"

Walker remained silent. He didn't really believe she expected an answer.

"Now that you have my undivided attention, what do you want?"

"The reason we are here is to provide protection for you until Mr. Franklin is captured."

"So far, Mr. Walker, the only thing you've provided is making my worst nightmare come true. I'm not sure how you are going to make that better."

A facial muscle jumped as he tightened his jaw. Again he counted slowly to ten.

———

So Marshal Trey Walker likes to be in control at all times. Well, wasn't this going to be an interesting power struggle. After her ordeal with Mark, she had never again let anyone control her life. Her momentary lapse at the mention of Mark's name was just that, a momentary lapse.

She had been the one to turn in Mark to the police when she discovered the paperwork that showed him skimming money from his clients. Not only did Mark blame her for being disloyal, but he had tried to run her over the night before the trial. She had been lucky to survive, and she knew it.

She would never allow Mark or any man to ever again control her life or feelings. She liked where she was at in her life now and she intended to continue down that path. Someday there could be room for a man, but she had yet to meet one who wanted to be her equal in a relationship.

Logan's smile was beginning to diminish slightly and was slowly replaced by a puzzled look. He glanced from Sandra to Walker, perhaps finally cluing in on the tension.

Sandra continued to watch Walker, waiting for his answer. If she didn't know better, she would think he was counting to ten. He cleared his throat.

"Ms. Johnson, we take death threats seriously." He paused. "Mark Franklin tried to kill you before the trial. On a scale of one to ten as to how dangerous he is, we believe him to be at ten plus."

Sandra shuddered. The events from three years ago had changed her life forever. She still had occasional nightmares.

Nightmares that woke her up with a racing heart and a need to change out of her sweat-soaked pajamas.

"So, where do we go from here, gentlemen?" Sandra practiced the slow breathing her counselor had taught her whenever her anxieties surfaced.

"This is a pretty standard operation. We simply accompany you as you go about your daily life, until we have word that Franklin has been captured."

"Does that mean you start trailing me as soon as I leave my house in the morning and stick with me until I get back at night?"

The question seemed to make Walker a little uncomfortable as a slight twitch appeared near his right eye.

"Not exactly."

Chapter 2

Sandra was ready to scream. The robotic responses from him made her want to scratch his eyes out. "Why do I have to pull the answers out of you, Mr. Walker? Can't you give me the full details in one breath instead of breaking them up one word at a time? I really am bright enough to follow you."

"We have to physically be near you twenty-four hours a day until Franklin is caught. That means not only do we have to follow you, one of us has to be in the same car with you. We have to sleep at your place, and we have to eat with you. We do everything short of following you into the bathroom."

"Thank you. Now was that really all that hard? And the answer is no. You will not be staying at my house."

"You might find the situation amusing, Ms. Johnson, but I can assure you we take this quite seriously."

"I have no doubt, Mr. Walker, you do take this seriously and I guarantee I don't find this amusing. I've known you for what? Maybe five minutes? Even in that short time I picked up on how seriously you take *everything*. You should try relaxing once in a while."

He didn't even flinch. Logan turned and tapped Walker on the arm.

"Uh, boss. I don't think Ms. Johnson wants us here."

"Nobody ever wants us, Logan. But they don't have a choice. If they refuse, then they have to be taken to another place for protective services. The choice is totally up to them."

Sandra mulled over his comment trying to decide if he was bluffing. Did they have the authority to cart her off to never-never land because she refused their services?

Trey and Sandra eyed each other carefully. If they had been standing, they would have been circling each other like Sumo wrestlers, waiting for the opportunity to pin the other to the mat. Neither was going to let the other person have the upper hand. Their strong wills were both their best friends and their worst enemies.

Sandra bestowed a smile, that didn't reach her eyes, on Logan that clearly relaxed him. If the Marshals were only staying for a day or two, Sandra could probably handle having them around. Besides, she honestly wasn't keen on being by herself until Mark was captured. However, the two men in front of her didn't need to know that.

"Mr. Logan, I appreciate your concern over what I may or may not want. And please, call me Sandra." She blew out a long breath, eyeing Walker. "Okay. I'll let you to do your job."

Walker acknowledged her decision with a nod while Danny's excitement spilled over.

"Oh, that will be great, Ms. ....uh... Sandra. You won't even know we're around."

Sandra highly doubted that. Two men constantly underfoot at work and at home would be hard to ignore. One in particular, who had shown himself to be accident-prone. But she acknowledged his comment with a gracious smile.

When she turned her attention back to Walker, her smile

faded. She wanted him to know that her sentiments about him were not the same.

"I do know, Mr. Walker, that I have the right to refuse you and am under no obligation to have you take me anywhere I don't want to go. What I do is my God-given right as a citizen of the United States. Your browbeating tactics won't work on me." Sandra paused to take a breath. "However, I also know your job is to protect me, and I imagine that if I don't allow you in my car or my business or my home, you will be around every corner anyway. Since you will be underfoot regardless, I will give you permission to be with me as you see fit."

Walker's face was expressionless. "Now that we have that settled, we need to establish ground rules."

"Oh, joy, rules."

Ignoring her sarcasm, Walker continued. "One of us has to be with you at all times. One of us always enters a place before you do so we know who is in the building."

"Anything else? Will you need to taste my food for poison as well? I'd let you do that." She gave him her sweetest smile.

"There will be no trying to shake us so that you can go meet a lover."

"Not a problem, he usually has to shake his wife to come to my place."

Walker pulled back a little, disgust replacing his stoic expression.

Sandra shook her head. "That was a joke, Walker." She stood and they followed suit. "If you want to make yourself comfortable, you may, however, I need to return to my client."

"One more thing, Ms. Johnson."

"Yes, Mr. Walker?" Sandra no longer cared if her exasperation showed.

"I need the keys to your house. I need to check the layout and security."

"Fine." Sandra opened a drawer and dug her keys out. "Here's my house key." She took the key off her car ring and handed it to him. As their fingers touched, she was surprised to find his were warm. She had naturally assumed he was cold-blooded through and through.

"I gather you know where I live."

He nodded. "Logan will stay here with you while I go check your house."

She and Danny followed Walker out into the workout area and watched him as he walked out the front door of her business. Sandra leaned casually against the doorjamb of her office.

"Do you think I should have told him about my dog?"

———

SANDRA'S HOUSE wasn't large, but it sat on a large corner lot. The soft yellow house with white trim was older and was complimented by a comfortable front porch that held two white wicker rockers. The backyard appeared to be completely fenced.

Trey glanced around the neighborhood as he opened the screen door. He saw nothing out of the ordinary. The street was quiet and he knew most of the occupants were retired, with a sprinkling of young families. Sandra Johnson and a widower across the street from her were the only single people in a four-block radius.

He turned the key, heard the lock release and opened the door slowly. Out of habit, he listened for any unusual noises then slipped inside where he was greeted by silence. His eyes took a moment to adjust to the dimness of what turned out to be the family room. The blinds were closed keeping the daylight out, but enough light filtered through the edge of the blinds to allow him to find the light switch.

The switch triggered a lamp sitting on a nearby end table.

He froze. There had been a noise. He held his breath. The sound came again. *Was that a growl?*

Trey slowly turned to discover he had indeed heard growling. Each time he moved the growling grew louder. He took a few slow breaths in an attempt to calm his heart that was pounding against his ribs.

The German shepherd lay between the family room and what appeared to be a bedroom and was resting his head on his front legs. His ears were sticking straight up and his eyebrows were elevated. Trey was pretty certain the dog wouldn't think twice about tearing him from limb to limb. Although he'd been shot at, stabbed and had chased down many a bad guy, this was his worst fear now staring him down.

Trey was going to kill Johnson. "It's okay, boy. Your mama knows I'm here."

The dog responded with a low growl. Although the dog remained unmoving, Trey was convinced he would lunge at him if he took one more step. At least that meant Franklin probably wasn't in the house.

He slowly reached into his pocket to retrieve his cell phone. The dog raised his head and tilted it as Trey pulled the phone out. Again, Trey found himself holding his breath.

"It's okay boy. Good boy. I'm just going to call your mama and give her a piece of my mind."

Satisfied Trey wasn't going to do anything out of the ordinary, the dog resumed his resting position. He was the biggest German Shepherd Trey had ever seen. He had heard dogs could sense fear and right now his fear factor was off the charts. If the other agents back at the office knew he was shaking in his boots because of a mere dog there would be no living this down.

Logan finally answered his phone, providing Trey with a sense of relief and a little more control.

"Logan, put Ms. Johnson on the phone."

"She's busy right now with a client, Boss. I don't think she wants to be disturbed."

Trey gritted his teeth. He was in hell. That had to be the answer. "I don't care what or who she is with, put her on the phone."

"Well, I'll try, but I can't guarantee anything."

Words were being exchanged in the background, but Trey couldn't tell what was being said.

"She's real busy, boss."

"Put her on the phone, *now*." He said the words slow, deliberate and through gritted teeth. This time there was minimal background talking and then silence.

"'Walker, you have to respect my clients. I have a business to run. You just can't call me and expect I'll drop everything."

"You conveniently neglected to tell me that you had a dog."

"Oh, did I? You mean he wasn't in your little report? Well, you don't have to worry about Tiny."

"Tiny? You named that overgrown freak of a dog, Tiny?"

"Well, when I picked him, he was the runt of the litter. Who knew he'd grow up to be a monster? You should see how much food he eats."

Trey could hear the amusement in her voice. She was enjoying his discomfort too much and he was losing his patience too easily with this woman. He had known her for an hour and he was ready to take her over his lap and give her a good spanking like the juvenile way she was acting. Unfortunately, the thought of spanking her brought other images to mind that he quickly suppressed.

"Tell me what I should do. He won't stop growling at me."

"Is he standing up or lying down?"

"Lying down."

"Well, this is good. He likes you already."

"Cut the crap, Johnson. What do I need to do to stop him

from growling?" Trey couldn't help how he felt. His fear of dogs had him back to talking through gritted teeth.

"Oh, that's simple. Walk over to him slowly, using his name and hold out your hand."

"Is that so he'll have something to chew on?"

"Aren't you funny. No, of course not. He's as gentle as a lamb. That way he can sniff your scent and accept you into his house. Go ahead, try it."

Feeling like an idiot and glad once again others from the agency weren't witnessing this humiliating moment, Trey slowly took one step then another towards the dog.

"Tiny? It's okay, boy." Trey stopped. "He's getting louder. I don't think he likes me."

"Is he still lying down?"

"Yes."

"Well, then you're fine. I'd only be concerned if he had stood up. Then I would have told you to run."

"This is not funny, Johnson. I'm not in the mood to be mauled by your dog."

"Keep doing what I told you." She was no longer holding back the laughter.

Trey slowly put one foot in front of the other as he approached the dog. One step shy of reaching him, Tiny lifted his head and Trey froze.

"He lifted his head," he whispered.

Sandra whispered back. "He wants to sniff your scent. Put your hand out to him."

Trey closed his eyes, took a deep breath and did what she said. He felt Tiny's cold, wet nose in the palm of his hand and the next thing he knew the dog was licking the salt from his sweaty hand. With a sigh of relief, he opened his eyes and found the dog examining him. Tiny's head was cocked to one side with one eyebrow higher than the other as if puzzled.

"Good boy, Tiny. Good boy."

He patted him on the head awkwardly still not convinced the dog wouldn't leap for his throat.

"That worked. He stopped growling."

"Of course it worked, although he doesn't always have the best taste in people."

"Funny, Johnson, real funny." Trey turned off the phone and slipped it back into his pocket. "Okay, Tiny, why don't you go into the yard for awhile."

As if he knew what Trey was telling him, Tiny stood and trotted ahead of him through the kitchen and out the sliding back door Trey opened. He watched as Tiny immediately walked over to a bush and marked his territory.

Closing the slider, Trey took a small notepad and pen from his shirt pocket and started making notes. The slider had to be made more secure, the windows throughout the house could be easily pried open from the outside, and the front door needed a better dead bolt.

Although small, the house had two bedrooms and two bathrooms, one of which was inside the master bedroom. Fortunately she also had a full-sized couch that Logan could sleep on while Trey took the guest room.

Trey walked the perimeter of the backyard and let Tiny back into the house. The huge dog promptly returned to his place, where he appeared to guard the virtues of Sandra's bedroom. Trey pitied the man who tried to replace Tiny's position in Sandra's life.

———

SANDRA LET OUT the breath she hadn't realized she had been holding when Trey returned. He had been gone only an hour, but the amount of chaos Danny had managed during that time had been utterly astounding.

She had agreed to let Danny scope out her business for the sake of security. She had thought giving him an assignment would be a good way to keep him out of her hair while she worked with a client. Until he disappeared into the back room to check the exit door and returned carrying the door handle.

"We will definitely need to make the back door more secure." He nodded his head in all seriousness as he relayed the obvious. "Yep, any idiot could come through that way."

Sandra could only stare. She had to admit, he was definitely right about the idiot part. Within five minutes of the doorknob incident, he came out of her massage room with oil spilled down the front of his pants.

"Sorry, Sandra. I cleaned the oil up the best I could."

Cleaning up meant he had grabbed the first thing he found which was a stack of clean sheets, rather than the rags she kept on hand. He had bypassed the rags in front of him and walked the length of the room to where she stored the clean sheets.

She cleaned what she could before her next client, having to leave the rest for later.

Once she settled her client into a routine, Sandra took the sheets to the room where she housed the washer and dryer. In the midst of throwing the sheets into the washer, she heard a sickening crash from the exercise room.

She popped her head out to see a couple of weight disks lying on the floor and another one slowly circling until it, too, clanged to the floor. Millie Cleveland, who had been doing a set of weights, had stopped to stare at Danny. Sandra recognized the confusion on her face. The look was probably the same one she had on her own face.

"I don't even want to know how this happened." Sandra mumbled the thought to herself, but Danny heard and was quick to answer.

"Oh, it was actually quite simple."

Sandra raised her hand to stop any further explanation from him. "You could be the biggest help right now, Danny, by sitting over in the chair by the window. Read the newspaper or a magazine or stare out the window, I don't care, but don't leave that chair until Walker returns." She tried to muster a smile in an attempt to take some of the edge off. "Do you understand?"

"Yeah. But can't I help you clean this up first?"

"NO!" She took a deep breath and pressed her fingers to her temples trying to stem the headache waiting in the wings. "I mean, picking up these weights will only take a minute. I need to have you sit." She pointed to a chair. "Over there."

She watched him and made sure he was settled before she picked up the disks and placed them where they belonged. Millie Cleveland finished her set and Sandra ran her through the rest of her circuit training while keeping an eye on Danny.

Although she wasn't overly taken with Trey Walker, she was glad when he walked through the door. Danny was his responsibility again. No more babysitting for her.

"I see you're no worse for wear, Walker. Tiny left you in one piece." She couldn't help a smile as she recalled the phone call.

"I don't like surprises, Ms. Johnson. In the future you should keep that in mind."

"I'm hoping our future is short. Very short."

Danny stood when Trey walked through the door and once again appeared to be the eager puppy wanting to please whoever would let him. He rocked back and forth, foot to foot, waiting to insert his two cents in their conversation. Sandra had to admire his restraint. When Trey's attention wandered to Danny, she noted the puzzled look on his face as he took in Danny's oil-stained pants. Trey closed his eyes and rubbed his hands over his face.

"I know I shouldn't ask, but what the hell happened to your pants, Logan?"

"Well, I was doing what you told me to."

Sandra felt a bit sorry for Danny. He was such a mismatch with Walker, who obviously had no patience to teach him the ropes. On the other hand, after having been alone with Danny for an hour and the destruction he managed to cause, she couldn't really blame Walker for the frustration he was feeling.

Trey briefly shifted his eyes to Sandra as if afraid to ask the obvious question.

"And what did I ask you to do?"

"Well, you didn't really ask me, it was more implied. Since you checked the security at Sandra's house, I figured I should do the same here."

Danny was obviously pleased with himself. He had pulled himself up to his full stick-figured height of six feet. In that brief moment, he seemed sure of himself and Sandra saw a glimpse of the man he would become. On the other hand, Walker didn't seem to see the possibilities of Danny. He seemingly had no heartfelt understanding of the human nature. What a sad, lonely man he must be. How could you go through life without having any empathy or compassion towards another human?

"What's in your hand?"

"This?" Danny raised his hand revealing the doorknob to Sandra's back door. "I was checking the back door and it just came off. There'll have to be better locks."

Danny nodded his head much like he had done when he had shown the handle to Sandra. She bit her lip to keep from smiling, torn between feeling glad Danny was Walker's responsibility and feeling sorry he was Walker's responsibility.

Trey didn't seem impressed and closed his eyes. For the second time, Sandra wondered if he was counting to ten.

Opening his eyes, he finally addressed the obvious. "And your pants? What do you have on your pants?"

"Oh, that." Danny waved off the question. "I was checking Sandra's massage room and spilled massage oil." He snorted.

"Is there anything else he destroyed while I was gone?" Walker seemed reluctant to ask the question.

"He had a little problem with a few of my weights, but other than that, no." Sandra gave Danny a smile of reassurance. "He's only trying to do his job, Walker."

"His job was to simply stay with you and make sure you were safe."

Giving Walker her most brilliant smile, she responded, "And he did that with flying colors, don't you think?" Walker wasn't going to give anyone a break. He simply had a permanent frown on his face.

Chapter 3

That had been a close call. The motel Mark Franklin had slept at was quiet and off the main drag. A perfect spot to stay off the radar. Or so he had thought.

However, when he emerged from his room to continue his journey, he came face to face with two sheriffs. They walked toward him, hands resting on their holstered guns and he automatically assumed they were there for him. He briefly wondered if he could outrun them.

On second glance, he realized there were just two sheriffs. If the authorities had found him, there would have been a number of backups and guns drawn.

The sheriffs stepped around him as they continued down the walkway, barely making eye contact. They stopped four doors down, took up positions on either side of the door and released their guns from their holsters. One of them pounded on the door, yelling for a guy named Murray. Mark continued to watch the action as he unlocked the door of the stolen car.

Apparently this Murray guy wasn't willing to open the door nicely for the officers, so they kicked the door in and entered. Easing his frame into the car, Mark started the car and drove off, glad those two would be occupied for a while with a drug dealer or a thief.

He had escaped the prison only twenty-four hours earlier which meant they must have discovered he was gone by now.

Three years ago when he entered the prison, he had kept his distance from the other inmates. He wasn't one of them. He had simply taken what was rightfully his. His clients hadn't suffered. Their wealth had only grown because of him. What he had added to his nest egg he had earned. He had worked like a dog for those clients to find stock that would give them the best returns possible. None of them had complained when he delivered what he promised.

In the prison system you were treated the same by jail officers and inmates. The exception was if you were behind bars for harming kids. If that was the category you fell into, both jail officers and inmates gunned for you. You could be beaten senseless while a jail officer ignored the disorder.

Convictions of embezzling and attempted murder were tame in comparison. Because of that, he managed to stay under the radar and made damn sure he didn't draw attention to himself. Many of the men were hardcore lifers and had years of lifting weights to occupy their time. The last thing he wanted was for any of them to notice him.

Even though he kept from engaging with the other inmates, there was one who made a habit of sitting next to him at lunch every day. His name was Lincoln. Simply Lincoln. Mark didn't know or care if that was his first or last name. At first, Mark ignored him and didn't respond, letting him ramble about his ex-wife and three kids and the ins-and-outs of prison life. He was in for robbing a bank at gunpoint. His family had needed food.

But one day, Mark stopped ignoring Lincoln and started to listen. Lincoln had pointed out several times how much Mark and one of the guards were similar. Close to the same age, same build, same hair color. The only difference was in their mannerisms.

Lincoln nudged Mark on the arm and motioned to one of the guards. "That's him. Your twin."

Mark was surprised to see a guard who truly could have been one of his brothers. Mark watched as he walked among the chow tables making small talk with the prisoners.

"He's okay for a jail officer. All the inmates seem to like him. If we ever had a prison riot, he'd be the only one we'd let go. His name is Grier. Samuel Grier."

For the first time, Mark really focused on Lincoln. "Well, then maybe I should get to know him."

The decision to break out of prison hadn't formed in that moment, but Mark had always trusted his instincts. The fact that they looked so much alike he was sure could be used to his advantage. A few weeks later, he started contemplating how their resemblance could come in handy.

Over the next year and half, Mark studied Grier's movements. How he walked, how he used his hands when he talked, and even how he talked. For months, Mark practiced Grier's movements and mannerisms in the privacy of his cell. One day he tried them out on Lincoln.

"Man, you've got him down pat. If you had his uniform, you could walk out of here a free man."

Walking out a free man was exactly what Mark intended to do.

Mark pulled sunglasses over his eyes as the sun emerged from behind the clouds. He had his window open so he could breathe the fresh air.

Prison didn't have fresh air. Sure, they had gone outside to the exercise field, but that hadn't been true fresh air. The gray walls, slabs of concrete, dust and a barbed wire fence stifled the prison air.

Here, though, where he cruised down the backcountry roads, everything was fresh.

The green wheat sprouts gave the countryside the appearance of an endless lawn across the rolling fields. As he passed grazing horses and cows, he found he even enjoyed the smell of the fields.

In the small towns he passed through, there was the occasional smell of freshly mowed grass. He had missed a lot by working long hours in the corporate world. Outdoors for him had been strictly for running and maintaining his tan. The thought had never entered his mind to enjoy being outside. Now the outdoors stretched before him, welcoming him as he continued to his destination.

Mark had found Grier's routine easy to determine. And, with a few leading questions here and there over the year, Mark had been able to gather enough information from Grier to know just enough about his routine to help him escape.

Mark had followed the same routine to the letter. He retrieved Grier's lunch box and car keys from his locker, using the birth date of Grier's mother for the lock to gain access. There had been two other guards in the break room that he knew to be Mancetti and Paulson. Keeping his head lowered slightly so that the bill of his cap would cover his eyes better, he had exchanged greetings with them.

After wishing them a good evening, he had headed to the parking lot where he knew the exact location of Grier's car as well as the make and model. None of the other jail officers had been the wiser. The only person they saw and heard was Samuel Grier when he left that night.

He had dumped Grier's car not long after leaving the prison parking lot. The envelope of money and change of clothes that

Megan had left for him had been waiting down the road about ten miles at a little country church. They had been exactly where they were supposed to be, hidden behind a large rock surrounded by bushes.

In order to throw the cops off his trail, he had taken a bus out of Rockville, buying a ticket for the very last stop in the opposite direction from Sandra Johnson. He had exited at the midway point sometime around four in the morning. The owner of a vehicle in a well-to-do residential neighborhood had been nice enough to leave the car unlocked and a set of keys above the visor. He had dumped that car within a few hours. Now he was in a car courtesy of a corporate parking lot. Hopefully the owner wouldn't discover his or her car missing until closing hours.

He was sticking to country roads in order to avoid large groups of law enforcement. The trip would take longer, but that was okay. He had decided on a round about way to visit Sandra. He laughed out loud. He was one visitor she would regret ever setting eyes on. At least, for as long as he permitted her to live.

The traveling was easy. There wasn't a lot of traffic, just enough so he didn't stand out. The times he did meet a cop on the road, he didn't relax until he was sure they weren't going to whip around and come after him. As much as he would have liked to press the speed limit, he didn't dare attract attention to himself.

As the miles stretched between him and prison, he became more convinced he wouldn't have any problems paying a visit to Sandra before heading to Mexico. Hopefully while he was taking the less direct route, the cops would believe he had already skipped the country and the urgency to find him would diminish. Everyone's guard would be down including Sandra's. Then he could finish the job.

Chapter 4

For the better part of the evening, Sandra gathered up anything dear and precious and removed it from the vicinity of Danny. He was like having a toddler in the house. Everything had stayed intact so far and she wanted to keep it that way.

Sandra loved her cozy house. The place was intimate and manageable. Plus, the extra bedroom gave her the luxury of having her family or an occasional friend stay when they came to town.

Her kitchen had a slider door that, when left open, gave the impression that the kitchen extended into the outdoors. The large lot gave Tiny lots of room to stretch his legs. The garden window at the sink provided natural light and had a view of the side yard and street. A table for two occupied her one free wall.

The family room consisted of a full-sized sofa, a wing-backed chair, a desk for her computer, and a television. The sage green walls were warm and inviting.

Sandra had carefully thought out the placement of each piece of furniture so that more than one person could flow from room to room without bumping into something. The house wasn't designed, however, to accommodate her and two men, one of whom was a danger to anything breakable while the other seemed to take up any extra breathable space.

While Danny was eager to help out with dinner and play with the dog in the backyard, his counterpart spent his time on the computer or the phone. Whatever he was doing kept her from having to carry on a conversation with him, which was fine with her.

He paused long enough to eat the dinner she had prepared. His "thank you" seemed mechanical.

While Danny was an open book, Walker was tight-lipped. She wasn't sure if he really didn't have anything to say, or if he just wasn't sociable. Even Tiny gave up trying to capture his attention. Not that Walker was going to take a liking to a dog any time soon as Tiny did his best to try to get petted.

By the end of the evening, she was convinced her body pillow provided more warmth and personality than Walker. She couldn't imagine why someone who had his looks and a decent job couldn't muster a personality.

After dinner, Sandra spent some time on her own computer, doing bookwork for the business. Then she took Tiny for a walk. Walker sent Danny with her. Heaven forbid Walker should have to do something that would lead people to believe he was human, Sandra thought. His grunting comments and orders were getting old.

The late spring night was beautiful. The day had been exceptionally warm and although the evening was cooling down, it was still pleasant enough for people to sit on their porches. Sandra waved and said hello to everyone by name.

This neighborhood had been a blessing in disguise. Everyone was friendly and watched out for each other without a lot of gossip. Perhaps the variety of the ages of homeowners made the difference.

"So what's the story on Walker?"

They had walked Tiny a few blocks down the street before Sandra could no longer resist asking.

"What do you mean?"

Danny was holding Tiny's leash and for once Tiny was behaving. Usually Sandra felt as though she was being dragged down the street. Tiny must have decided to tone down his eagerness and be polite with the company.

"He seems...well... a little uptight."

"Oh, that. Well, he is."

Sandra laughed. You had to love it when someone spoke the truth. Danny laughed with her.

"We only met when we were assigned to you. Even though I've only been with him a few hours, I couldn't tell you how long he's been with the agency, if he is married, or if he has kids. He won't answer questions directly, especially personal. The only thing I've gathered is, like you said, he's uptight. Everything needs to be done by the book and he isn't exactly excited he got stuck with me."

Sandra was impressed by Danny's insight. Because of his awkwardness she had assumed his unease extended into every area of his life. Based on his insights on Walker, though, she might have to rethink that notion.

"I'm sure no matter who was with him, Danny, he wouldn't have been excited. I take him to be more of a loner."

"Perhaps."

Sandra saw the cat at the same moment Tiny did, which turned out to be way too late to warn Danny. Tiny took off after the cat, dragging Danny with him. If the darn thing hadn't hissed and run, Tiny would have ignored it, but running was a definite invitation to chase.

Danny ran behind Tiny, desperately yelling at him to stop. Sandra was impressed that he still had ahold of the leash. His free arm was flailing in an effort to maintain his balance. How he succeeded was simply a miracle. Sandra seriously doubted Danny outweighed Tiny by much, and when there was a cat involved, Tiny was a force to be reckoned with.

By the time Sandra caught up with them two blocks later at the base of an oak tree, Danny was leaning over his knees trying to catch his breath, while Tiny sat on his haunches, panting and looking quite pleased with himself for chasing the bad kitty up a tree.

"Oh, Tiny, why can't you behave?" Turning to Danny she couldn't keep the smile from her face. "Sorry about that, Danny. Usually I'm more attentive to the critter activity when we are out walking."

She bit her lip to keep from chuckling at the image of him being dragged down the street. Taking the leash she said, "Let's head back. I think both of you have had enough exercise for one night."

Straightening, Danny eyed Tiny carefully. "Next time at least give me a warning, boy. A bark. Something."

By the time they walked through the front door, they were both chuckling over the situation. Walker scowled at them.

"Could you keep the noise down?"

The easy smiles on Sandra and Danny's faces dissolved.

"Excuse me?" Sandra was taken aback at the gall of Trey Walker. He was in her house, asking her to keep the noise down.

"I said, could you keep the noise down. I'm trying to get some work done."

"That's it." Sandra's patience had ended. "I'm tired of your attitude. I didn't sign on to have your holier-than-thou attitude in my home." She opened the door and waved her arm to the outside. "Out. Both of you."

"That's not possible."

"Sure it is, Walker. You reverse the order in which you

entered my premises. Close up your damn computer, grab your bag and walk out the door. It isn't rocket science."

Walker unfolded himself from the couch and stood. "We can't leave you alone, Ms. Johnson. We've been assigned to protect you and under no circumstances will we be leaving."

The attitude Troy Walker had brought with him when he showed up today at her gym had slowly eaten away at Sandra's patience. Red hair aside, she liked to be in control of her emotions. What was it about this stranger that made her feel like giving in to a full-blown outburst of temper?

She took a deep breath and walked to the bedroom where Walker had dumped his things. Grabbing his bag, she retraced her steps and heaved the heavy duffel out the door. Walking to the couch, she grabbed Danny's bag and did the same.

"Fine," she told Walker. "You can start by protecting me from your pissy attitude and getting your ass out of my house. I'll be damned if anyone comes into my home and starts to tell me what I can and can't do."

Sandra stood at the open door, one hand on the knob and the other hand on her hip. Although her anger was directed at Walker, she detected confusion on Danny's face. For a moment when they had been walking Tiny, she had seen the agent he would become. The situation made her even angrier with Walker for what he couldn't see right in front of him.

Walker was in front of Sandra in three strides requiring her to peer up. She forced herself not to step back. She refused to let him think he could intimidate her. He had removed his suit jacket and tie at some point in the evening. His sleeves were rolled up, and a few of his buttons were undone. His stark white shirt stood out against his sun-darkened skin. His persona seemed more menacing than when he was in Marshall uniform.

Any other person would have cowered at his immense presence in such a small space. If Sandra had learned anything from her experience with Mark, it was that you shouldn't allow anyone to dictate how you could live your life. That included Mr. Walker trying to run over her with his words or his position.

"Logan, get our bags."

"Danny, don't do it. I'm done with you guys and you're leaving."

Neither Walker nor Sandra took their eyes off each other.

"Logan, as your superior, you will do as I say."

"Yes, sir."

As much as Sandra would have liked to muscle them both out the door, she knew that was physically impossible. Danny returned with the bags and Walker removed her hand from the doorknob, then closed and bolted the door.

"That wasn't a wise idea to stand in an open doorway when there's reason to believe someone is out to kill you. Open doors make you an easy target.'

"You didn't seem to have that concern earlier when I took Tiny for a walk."

"You had Logan with you and that dog."

"Neither of which can stop a bullet."

"True enough, but then I don't think Franklin has had time to make it here."

Sandra wanted to scream. Walker was an outright bully and he was pushing her buttons and she was letting him. She took a deep breath and let it out slowly in effort to lower her blood pressure.

"You must have loads of friends, Walker. What with your charming personality and that sense of humor of yours, you must be the hit of every party."

"I do happen to have loads of friends, none of whom have ever questioned my sense of humor."

Although his expression didn't change, something in his eyes shifted for a fraction of a second. Hidden under his façade of all business and no play, there might actually beat the heart of a human being. Perhaps blood did run through his veins rather than the ice she had imagined under the cold exterior.

"Somehow I highly doubt that. Now, if you both would pack up and remove yourself from my house, I would like to go to bed."

"As I said before, we can't do that. Only my superior can order me off this case."

"So give me his number and I'll call him. I would like to tell him how obnoxious you are, and that I recommend they fire you as well."

"She's a woman, and I doubt you'd get very far. Someone needs to be with you twenty-four seven and no one else is available. You're stuck with us."

"Fine, if you are going to stay, then I'll leave." Sandra turned to leave only to be stopped when Walker grabbed her by the arm.

She froze and stared at the hand wrapped around her arm. The warm fingers clamped around her upper arm confirmed what she had been thinking moments ago. He indeed had a beating heart that drove warm blood pulsing through his body. Even with five inches of space between them, she could feel his body heat.

Her own heart responded with a quickened beat and heat was slowly spreading in the pit of her stomach.

Why she had suddenly become aware of him as a man at that moment, she wasn't sure. Was it because of the warm touch or his obvious strength?

The grip on her arm was firm enough to detain her, but not enough to hurt her. She could tell he was keeping himself in check. That was another first. First believing he might have a sense of humor and now realizing that he was controlling his strength so he wouldn't hurt her.

She slowly moved her eyes along his arm to the rolled-up sleeve of his white shirt. His arm had a lot of dark hair and her fingers itched to touch the hair and see if it was soft or coarse.

She noted the muscles on his forearm, emphasized by his grip. Without even having to touch him, she knew he was hard as steel. All over. If those muscles were so well developed, she could only imagine what the rest of his body was like. She shuddered and felt her face start to heat up.

Her imagination became fixated on her hands creeping under his shirt and touching what she knew would be a taut belly. She felt numb at the thought of tracing a finger down to the top of his pants and taking her time in unbuckling his belt. Her heart raced at the thought of running her fingers along the band of his pants and knowing his skin would be soft and warm.

She shook her head and licked her lips in an attempt erase the images and move back into reality. However, when she made eye contact with him that proved to be a mistake. The steel-blue eyes stole the breath from the depths of her lungs. Sandra wasn't sure if Walker's soul was reflected in his eyes, but she recognized he was human and not the robotic person he portrayed.

His eyes were no longer hard and unrelenting. The demanding command once reflected in them had been replaced by a genuine emotion. She recognized the look of lust and a fire ignited in her belly at the thought that she was responsible for his response. She wondered if he had been taken aback by the skin-to-skin contact as well. Perhaps he had been surprised to find she, too, was made of flesh and blood.

He let go of her arm when he seemed to realize she was no longer struggling to step away. Sandra watch his eyes change back to what she had become accustomed to. A man who was in charge; a man no one should mess with. Had she been mistaken? Had she seen a human spark in this man who did things by the book? She rubbed at her arm where he had been holding her and treasured the warmth his contact had left.

"Did I hurt you?" He watched her rub the spot.

Sandra blinked. She could have sworn his voice had softened a bit. Perhaps that was as close to an apology as she would receive. "No."

His shoulders relaxed some, obviously relieved. "You have to understand, Ms. Johnson, I can't allow you to leave."

"If I stay or let you stay, there have to be some additional ground rules." She waited for him to say something and when he simply folded his arms across his chest as if waiting patiently, she ventured forward. "This is my house. You're not to tell me what and when I can do something. My schedule isn't hard to follow and it isn't unreasonable. I expect to be treated with respect. The same goes for when you are at my business."

"On one condition."

"Lord, of course you would have a condition. It's like you need to always have the last word." Exasperated and tired, she let out a sigh. "What would that be?"

"That you follow all of our safety precautions, no questions asked."

Chapter 5

Sandra tossed and turned for over an hour after going to bed. Normally sleep came quickly. The physical demands of her job were a perfect antidote to insomnia. She tried to convince herself that sleep eluded her because of having two extra people in the house. Men she didn't know. Any disruption in your schedule could be hard, but having two U.S. Marshals assigned to you and sharing your day-to-day life wasn't at all appealing.

She kept plenty busy between her work as well as programs in the community. Keeping busy had been the ticket she had needed to move forward after her release from rehab. Once she decided to take the steps to move on, she had done them quickly. Finding a new community in which to start over had done a lot to bolster her self-esteem. The move had put her closer to her family, but not so close that her mom could pop in whenever she wanted.

And now this. She sighed. She had thought she was done with drama. Part of her should have realized Mark wouldn't permit that to happen.

Sandra rolled over on her side, rearranging the pillow in an attempt to settle into the perfect spot that would aid her in falling asleep. She hugged the body pillow close to her chest for comfort. An ache still surfaced whenever she took time to remember what could have been. Like so many others, she had wanted the happy ending and still felt stupid for not seeing the person Mark truly was. She wasn't sure if she could ever really trust again. She was scared now of trusting her own judgment. Relationships with friends weren't the problem. Having a relationship with the opposite sex seemed to be.

And now she had two men under her roof. She had to child-proof her house for one and the other had about as much personality as the badge he flashed.

Not surprisingly, Walker had taken the bedroom and Danny had ended up on the couch with legs and arms dangling everywhere. Walker liked to accommodate only himself from what Sandra had observed over the past few hours.

The temporary emotion that had appeared in his eyes during their confrontation had given her some hope that he would let his guard down. He had shown more passion in that moment than Sandra would have believed otherwise. But when he had shut the emotion down and had gone back to being his irritating self, Sandra had retreated to her bedroom.

No wonder she had trouble falling asleep. The man was infuriating and had jumped on her last nerve in less than a day.

She took some more deep breaths and let them out slowly, once again trying to relax. She flipped onto her back and stared at the ceiling trying to decide if she should read for a little while. Tiny was in his usual spot, sprawled on the floor next to the bed, softly snoring.

The one bright spot of the evening had been when she had heard raised voices outside her bedroom door. Still holding a hand towel, she opened her door to see what the commotion was about. She had half-expected to see a physical fight in progress based on the noise, but instead, Walker had come out of the bathroom wiping toothpaste off the side of his face. His usual scowl was in place. He growled and walked into the bedroom.

"Sorry, Boss." Danny popped out of the bathroom holding his toothbrush. He looked at Sandra and reported, "I spit toothpaste on him."

Sandra burst out laughing causing Walker to return and close the bedroom door. He probably would have slammed the door if the carpet weren't so thick. A smile broke across Danny's face. With the door closed, he didn't have to worry about Walker's continued wrath.

Sandra knew that sleep was eluding her because of Walker. She wasn't even sure what she was most aggravated about. The fact that he was so heavy handed about protecting her or that she had thought for a second there was anything remotely human lurking in the depths of his soul.

Reflecting over the afternoon and evening, she was a little amazed that Walker hadn't insisted on taking over her room. He would have known from scouting the house that not only did her room have a private bathroom, but a king size bed as well.

A quick flash of him in her bed made her pulse leap and her body heat up again causing the fire pit in her stomach to flame. With more detail than she realized she had retained, she remembered the warmth and strength of his fingers wrapped around her arm. She remembered how his silver watch had accentuated the dark hair covering his tanned arm. She had no problem imagining those hands skimming over her skin, leaving a trail of heat from his fingers.

Throwing the covers off, Sandra slid out of bed, stepping over Tiny. The thumping of his tail was his only acknowledgement of her movement.

The cool air was refreshing against her skin. Her feet sank

into the softness of the carpet as she made her way to the bathroom. She splashed cool water on her face hoping to put an end to the path of betrayal her mind had set out on. As she patted the moisture off, she examined her reflection in the mirror. She had obviously completely lost her flippin' mind.

Padding back to bed, she was determined to go to sleep. She realized energy was being wasted on a man who, if the good Lord permitted, would be packed and on his way out of her life in the morning. With the thought of Mark being captured and the Marshals out of her hair firmly planted in her head, she finally fell asleep.

———

ONE MOMENT the fog was thick and she couldn't see what was in front of her. The next moment the fog was a light, swirling mist. Different apparitions faded in and out, none of them with definitive forms. The only constant occurrence was a distant light reflected in the mist that contributed to the eeriness of her surroundings.

She wasn't sure where she was, but knew she didn't want to be here. She took each step with care for fear that she would be swallowed up by some mystical hole.

She heard a noise ahead. "Who's there?"

Peering into the mist and darkness, she tried desperately to make out something or someone. Her heart was racing in fear. The fear constricted her throat.

She brushed at the mist and finally could see someone walking towards her.

Initially there weren't any distinct characteristics, but as the person continued towards her, the mist started clinging to their features. Sandra cocked her head to one side, squinting in hopes she could get a clear picture.

The person was a lot taller than she was. With each step, his features became clearer as the mist continued to define the man in front of her. Fear threaded through her body and her feet felt like lead.

Relief swept through her when the man who emerged was Trey Walker. She felt silly for having let the darkness and the mist frighten her. But now she knew she was safe. Trey was there to protect her.

He smiled at her and she smiled in return, so thankful that her fear hadn't been justified. He had a nice smile that warmed her.

She started walking a little faster to him. He reached a hand out and joy flooded her heart and soul. Only steps now from being embraced by him, her steps faltered until she stopped in her tracks. Something wasn't right. She watched as Trey's smiling face slowly transformed into a sneer on Mark Franklin's face. Disgust was evident in his eyes.

"Trey, where are you?"

This wasn't right. Mark was in jail. Frantically, she scanned for Trey, turning in the mist quickly. Where had he gone? He wouldn't abandon her. He was there to protect her. He had promised that nothing would happen to her.

As she once again faced Mark, she realized why she had experienced the earlier fear. Her anxieties rushed to the surface and terror gripped her heart. Catching her breath was becoming more difficult.

There was no longer a sneer on his face. Instead, he was laughing. A laugh that sent chills through her body as she backed away from him. The outstretched hand that had been beckoning her now held a knife. He raised the knife over his head. Sandra screamed and started running. Every time she glanced behind her, though, Mark was right there. She couldn't seem to put any distance between them.

SLEEP ELUDED TREY AS WELL. He was use to a king bed for his body frame. The double bed he was in wasn't giving him room to spread out. He knew Sandra was nice and cozy in her king size bed. Maybe he should have insisted on taking her room. At least that way he wouldn't have had to endure Logan spitting on him.

As much as he would have liked to guilt her out of her room, he knew he could never really have done that. He could be hard-nosed at times and a jerk when necessary, but his mom had taught him to be a gentleman and no matter how infuriating the woman was, you always treated them like a lady.

Infuriating was a good description of Sandra Johnson, he thought. On the other cases where he had been assigned to protect an individual, they had been thankful. None of them had questioned his authority. They had been willing to be told what to do, including staying low until everything was under control. But not Sandra Johnson. No sir, she had to question him about everything.

Her point about the jail system was understandable, but she would never hear him say that. Until something goes wrong, you aren't always aware there was a need for a fix. You can anticipate a lot of things like riots or fights among the inmates, but until someone escapes by impersonating a jail officer, the system's radar is broken.

There were definite procedures in place if an inmate appeared to be ill. If the jail officer had followed them, Franklin would still be behind bars.

Once more trying to find a comfortable position, Trey thought about the few aggravating hours he had spent with Johnson. Of course, he couldn't blame everything on her that had frustrated him. Logan had become Trey's biggest irritation. He was more of a hindrance then an asset. Logan's specialty was in researching leads, either through the computer or by foot-work. He took care of the tedious details and tasks on cases the agency was working on. His work was what the attorneys needed to make cases stick and convict the bad guys.

Recently, though, the agency had established a mentoring program where everyone had a chance to spend time in the field. The program was an attempt to assist the desk agents in keeping hands-on with current methods used in the field as well as for the field agents to better understand what the desk agents received on the other end and how they processed details. Incorporating this method had already shown improvement in the turn around of cases.

Trey had not been in favor of the program and had been very vocal about that for exactly the reason he was experiencing. He knew every agent had extensive training, but after only a day with Logan, he wondered how Logan had made it through the physical program. He must be one hell of a computer whiz.

Trey had extensive experience on hardcore cases involving drug dealers and kidnappings. Witness protection cases, on the other hand, were usually low-key and gave an agent a breather from the intensity of the other assignments. They weren't his favorite, but he understood the logic of not burning agents out.

At this point, he could only hope he would get the call advising him they had caught Franklin. He could pass Logan onto someone else then. When Franklin was caught, Trey could move on to his next job without Logan and Sandra Johnson.

As mule headed as she was, he had to admire her determination to survive. He replayed their confrontation at the front door. She had done a good job of keeping her feelings in check until that moment. The emotional trauma she kept buried had surfaced in anger. Trey didn't blame her for her reaction. Her response was normal and expected.

What he hadn't expected was his reaction when he restrained her to keep from leaving. His body had betrayed him when they were mere inches from each other. The feeling was something so primal he felt as if he had been kicked in the gut. He had smelled the outdoor freshness still clinging to her from the walk. Her eyes had turned dark green with anger reflecting her fire and determination.

When his eyes had wandered to her mouth, he had come close to dragging her to him. Her lips were full and had been opened slightly and his lips had gone numb with the need to taste hers.

To be so fully aware of the woman he was there to protect, at a moment when he needed to concentrate on the job at hand, had been a first for him. But he couldn't deny his physical reaction. Even now, as he thought of her and those eyes and that mouth, his body responded. Frustrated, he turned on the light and read.

Trey woke suddenly and was out of bed in seconds, on his feet with gun in hand. His frame was flat against the wall next to the door. Something wasn't right. He had left his door open before going to bed and waited for the sound that had woken him.

The noise came again and sounded like moaning. He relaxed a little and proceeded to peer around the doorway to look at the couch, expecting to find Logan thrashing about. But he was sound asleep and quiet. One foot was on the floor and the other was resting over the edge of the couch. His arms were in similar positions.

Trey rubbed his chin. Logan appeared to be past whatever passionate dream or nightmare he had been having. He lowered his gun and turned back to bed hoping sleep would return quickly. The groan came again, this time louder and sounding more desperate.

Stepping outside his door, he snuck towards Sandra's door. He opened it slowly and glanced in. She was tossing and turning and appeared to be twisted in the blankets. Trey watched her for a few moments hoping she would calm down soon.

Instead, she started muttering. She seemed desperate to escape from something or someone. She was obviously agitated. Trey rubbed the back of his neck and realized whatever nightmare she was having didn't seem as if it was going to end soon. He opened the door enough so he could ease through the opening. As he stepped into the room, he heard a familiar growl. He stopped. Sandra could talk all she wanted about what a great dog Tiny was, but Trey still didn't trust the dog not to attack him.

"It's okay, boy, I came to help your mama." Surprisingly his excuse seemed to satisfy Tiny and he settled down once again.

Trey made his way over to the bed, gingerly stepping over Tiny, hoping he wouldn't have to wake her. He had heard that you shouldn't wake someone from a nightmare. Whatever was plaguing her, though, didn't seem to be going away and she was becoming more agitated by the second. He sat on the edge of the bed, placed his gun on the end table and started talking softly to her.

"Sandra, wake up, you're having a bad dream." He grabbed her hands as she appeared to be trying to push something away hoping the physical contact would break through. Instead her frantic struggle intensified as her panic rose.

"Sandra. Sandra. It's okay. You're okay. You're safe."

His last comment seemed to finally penetrate. She stopped struggling. In the dim light provided by the backyard light seeping through her blinds, Trey saw her eyes open.

In the next instant, the woman he had found so irritating not two hours earlier was clinging to him and shaking uncontrollably. She was breathing hard as if she had run a race.

He tentatively placed a hand on her back, not sure if she would scream or push him away. When neither of those happened, his arms closed around her and she pressed herself closer. He surprised himself when he started rubbing her back and providing words of comfort.

Where'd those words come from?

Even in the dimness of the room before she launched herself at him, he had noted how her pajama top, held up simply by thin straps, hugged her curves. The material was silky to the touch as was her skin, he discovered, when the top rode up enough that his hands made contact with her back.

The talk he had given himself earlier didn't seem to be working. The longer she stayed in his arms, the harder it was for him to keep the job strictly business.

She fit so well wrapped in his arms and he was enjoying the feeling of holding her more than he should. Everything about her was soft and warm and soothing to his senses. Her hair, which had been pulled back when he met her, was loose and wild from her sleep. Her halo of hair was crazy sexy and if he turned his head, he could easily bury his nose in the curls which would definitely lead to kissing her at that soft spot below her ear. The need to explore was overwhelming and he was having a hard time stomping down his physical response to her.

He mentally cleared the images from his mind and refocused on the business at hand. He was here to protect her. Only to protect her. He reminded himself that she was frustrating at best and had no respect for authority. Maybe his mother was right. If he was having this kind of reaction to a woman whom he would rather strangle then make nice with, perhaps he should start dating again.

Her shaking subsided after about five minutes. By that time, Trey had finally managed to readjust his thinking and return to Marshal mode. When she did make a move to withdraw from him, Trey pulled a little away to see how she was coping.

"Are you okay?"

"I think so."

"What was your nightmare about?"

She stared at his chest. "You."

"Me? You were having a bad dream about me?"

Was he really so dreadful that people were having bad dreams about him? He knew he came across as a hard-nosed, by-the-book agent and wasn't exactly sociable, but work was work and play was play.

As if she had suddenly realized how close in physical proximity they were, Sandra slipped her hands off his arms and scooted back to lean against the headboard. She drew her knees up, hugging them to her chest, showing both her vulnerability and the need to protect herself. Trey felt the loss of the human contact and warmth to the very depth of his soul. The feeling caught him unaware. He shrugged off the emotion chalking it up, once again, to the dry spell between girlfriends.

"Well, not exactly about you. You were in the dream."

"Go on." He felt relief that at least he wasn't the cause of her nightmare.

"There was fog and I was scared because I couldn't see anything. Then out of the fog appeared a man. At first the image looked like you, but as I continued to walk towards you, your face turned into Mark's."

"Franklin?"

"Yes. His hand was outstretched to me, but he held a knife. I took off running, but the distance between us grew shorter."

"So that's what I woke you up from, trying to run away from Franklin?"

Sandra nodded.

Trey couldn't begin to imagine the terror she had gone through. The report he had read had been as detailed as any other. But the recount of her dream brought back the image from the picture he had seen of her lying in a hospital bed, hooked up, bruised and broken and unrecognizable after being hit by Franklin's car. How or why she had lived after the impact, God only knew.

After meeting her, though, he had a better understanding. She was a determined woman. A woman who wasn't going to let anything or anyone decide how her life would unfold.

He believed his first impression of her was right on the money. This was a woman who had high values and would see they were met. Those values were so important that she expected those around her to hold the same. When she had found out Franklin had screwed his clients, she didn't stand back and watch. The injustice of Franklin's actions had affected the very heart of this woman, and even the man she was set to marry couldn't stand in the way of what she believed in and held true.

"Are you sure you're okay now?"

"I think so." Sandra had been examining her fingernails up until then, her chin resting on her knees. She viewed him through her eyelashes. "You must think I'm such a wimp to be scared by a dream."

"Lady, after what you endured three years ago, I'd be scared of your dream."

This prompted a soft laugh from Sandra.

"Can I get you anything? Water? Crackers? Liquor?"

"Funny. You should do that more often."

"What?"

"Show your sense of humor. A smile wouldn't hurt either."

Trey shrugged. "When I'm on assignment, I'm all business. I just wanted to lighten the mood a little to help you relax."

She studied him for a moment, a slight smile still on her face. "Thanks. It worked. And I must admit it was nice to see a more human side to you."

"Tomorrow morning when we meet again, you'll think this was a dream. I'll be back to my bad-ass ways."

"You can't get off that easy. Believe me, I'll remember."

"Seriously, though, is there anything I can get for you?"

"No." She waved him off as she started settling back into bed.

He stood up and helped untangle her blankets catching a glimpse of a well-developed leg.

"I'll try to go back to sleep now. Thanks for coming to my rescue." She gave him another smile before settling her head on her pillow.

"You're welcome," he said softly. He watched her a moment longer to assure himself that she was truly going to go to sleep before he grabbed his gun and turned to leave.

"Trey?"

"Yeah?" He was at the door with his hand on the knob. This was the first time she had called him by his first name and hearing that startled him.

"Would you leave the door open?"

"Sure."

Chapter 6

Sandra didn't have any difficulty falling back to sleep, perhaps because of the exhaustion of the dream. She did dream again, but this time none of the dreams included Mark. When she woke, there was with a smile on her face. The smile remained as she finished dressing for her morning run.

"Come on Tiny, time for you to go water the bushes."

Emerging from her room, she could hear the shower going in the other bathroom and noticed the smell of fresh-brewed coffee. What a change to have coffee waiting for her.

Rounding the corner to the kitchen, she found Trey's large body seemingly taking up the whole kitchen even while sitting at the table.

"Morning."

"Morning." Yep, there was good ole' Trey back this morning. The thought only made her smile broaden.

She opened the back door and let Tiny out. As she did every morning, she stood at the door and watched him run the fence line doing his perimeter check. Only once did he bark when he discovered a squirrel poised for flight under the large oak tree. The squirrel hurried up the tree for safety as Tiny lunged towards him. Then as happened most mornings, the squirrel noisily scolded Tiny as he marked the tree. This was the same routine every morning. The squirrel ran and Tiny gave him a literal piss-on-you attitude.

She always laughed at this interaction.

"Come back in, Tiny. Time for our run."

"Run?"

Tiny's feet hit the kitchen floor and he slid a little on the linoleum, his paws wet from the dew on the grass. His nails scraped the floor as he steadied himself, his attention focused entirely on Sandra. She retrieved the leash from the hook next to the door and fastened the strap on his collar.

"Yes, a run. This is the only time during the day when I can get my cardio. Is that going to be a problem?"

She threw the question down like a gauntlet and waited to see if he would rise to the challenge or try to convince her to skip her routine until Mark was caught. She expected him to choose the latter and then time would be wasted as he gave an argument as to why. Walker held her eyes as he seemed to contemplate his decision.

"No, not a problem. If you give me a minute, I'll change and join you."

Pushing back the chair, he stood and Sandra once again felt as if her house had shrunk. When her family or friends visited, the house never felt this small, but his size seemed to dominate her space. She refrained from stepping away from him. She didn't want him to think he could intimidate her physically.

"Okay."

In less than five minutes they were out the door and Sandra led him on one of her favorite routes. They wound through the quiet streets of her neighborhood and ended up at a large park. Sandra released Tiny from his leash, knowing he would stick close by, while he took the opportunity to explore the abundant smells of the park. The trees and bushes were in their glory, full and green, welcoming the spring day. The morning air was crisp and a slight breeze had the leaves whispering in the trees above them. The path wound through the park and, for a while, Sandra could escape the recent upheaval in her life and even manage to relax in the company of Trey Walker.

There was no conversation between them. None seemed to be necessary. The silence was companionable which surprised her since they had been butting heads from the moment they met. Perhaps they were better off avoiding conversation alto-gether. If only that were possible.

Sandra knew under different circumstances Walker could have easily out run her. He was stronger and leaner and seemed to run effortlessly. She wasn't struggling but, as usual, she didn't hold back. Sweat trickled down her face and neck, which felt good. Her runs had become a cleansing ritual that helped put her head in the right frame of mind for the day as well as for fitness purposes.

When she had first started running after the accident, the motions had been slow and painful, only managing a few running steps at a time on her walks. She had been a runner for years, but the physical pain was a constant reminder of being hit by a car, making the emotional pain harder to overcome.

Through counseling, she gained emotional strength. As her body continued healing, the physical pain lessened and her physical strength increased. Her morning runs became longer and she began to use that time for meditation. Each route had different benefits depending on what she felt she needed for the day. The route she was using today was one she used for calm. She really needed her calm reinstated. The park and trees put her in a place of peace and serenity. Today was no exception even with Trey tagging along. This was exactly what she needed after the nightmare the night before.

"That was impressive."

"What was?"

They were cooling down outside her house. Sandra was using the steps to stretch her calves and legs. Her breathing was almost back to normal and she was already running her daily schedule through her head.

"The run. I know fitness is your business and livelihood, but not everyone will push himself the way you do. Unless that was for my benefit."

"Wow. Really? Believe it or not, there are things that don't revolve around you. Hard to imagine why the women aren't knocking down your door."

"Who says they aren't?"

Finished with her stretching, she stood and started up the stairs of her house. "Are they?"

"I do okay."

"That sounds like a "no" to me."

"You don't know anything about me."

She faced him and found him on the bottom step, putting them at eye level.

"And you don't know anything about me. You've had access to only a small portion of my life. What you saw in print is a minimal part."

She hoped he received the message loud and clear. If he didn't want to be analyzed than he shouldn't try the same on her.

"I just know when a person has been through the terror you have been, that it leaves emotional scars."

Sandra paused at the front door, her hand on the knob, and turned a little as if she wanted to respond. Tiny waited for her to open the door, and when she didn't, he obediently sat to wait, ears perked and tongue hanging out.

"And I also know," Trey continued softly, "that regardless of the situation, when you lose a baby on top of what you've gone through, a part of you never heals."

She closed her eyes. When she opened them, she let Tiny and herself into the house without responding.

———

WALKER WATCHED her escape into the house and felt like kicking himself for bringing up the baby. Most agents would have only concentrated on what Franklin had done and not have read any further. But Walker liked detail and had thoroughly read the report. He wanted to know Sandra's frame of mind.

The hospital report had listed her injuries and surgeries, and buried at the bottom where the information could have been easily missed, was the fact she had been almost three months pregnant. Somehow she had survived and had lived through the hell of what he had no doubt would have been intense physical therapy in order to be physically better. However, there had been no way for a baby to survive the impact Sandra had taken.

A stab of sadness and sorrow for her had momentary pierced his core when he had read of her loss. His exterior was tough and he proved that continuously, but there were some things that still could slip under his skin even when he didn't know the person.

There were the husbands who murdered their pregnant wives or mothers who drowned their children. The defenselessness of their victims and how they took advantage of that vulnerability, truly showed what cowards they were. In those cases, the death penalty was too good for them as far as Trey was concerned. They needed to rot in hell. Slowly.

Although he didn't have kids of his own, he doted on his nieces and nephew and perhaps was more sensitive to the situation than he might have otherwise been, particularly in view of what he did for a living. Or maybe knowing how much Sandra had endured after her fiancée betrayal. Franklin's attempt on her life and then losing a baby on top of all of it seemed especially cruel.

Walker made short work of his shower and walked into the kitchen as Sandra let Tiny out the backslider. She was in a robe and her hair was still wet from her shower. Not bothering to acknowledge him, she walked past him to her bedroom.

He poured himself another cup of coffee. Logan was sitting on the edge of the sofa watching some morning news show, seemingly oblivious to the tension that had fallen over the house.

Trey was sitting at the table browsing through his computer when Sandra once again came into the kitchen. Still ignoring him, she poured a bowl of cereal and a cup of coffee. Rather than sit at the table with him, she wandered back through the family room and out the front door.

Shit! Why couldn't she stay put?

"Logan!"

There was no answer so Trey went to find him. The bathroom door was closed. He ran a hand through his hair and swore under his breath. Grabbing his jacket he stepped out onto the small porch where he found her, feet propped up on the railing, eating the cereal with slow deliberate bites seemingly lost in thought.

"Do I really need to remind you that one of us must be with you at all times?"

She continued eating, not bothering to respond. That didn't surprise him and perhaps he deserved her silence.

The street was quiet except for birds chirping. A squirrel darted across the street, pausing to sit up, his tail curved in a question mark as he listened for anything out of the ordinary. Satisfied all was well, he continued on his journey with his fluffy tail floating behind as he effortlessly bounced across the dew-laden lawns and jumped onto the nearest tree trunk.

Leaning against the porch column, Trey sipped his coffee and watched Sandra as she continued to eat and take in the morning stillness. She was dressed for work in a matching athletic jacket and pants. The pants were grey with a contrast of white down the sides elongating her already long legs. Those legs could drive a man insane as he recalled the glimpse he had seen of them last night.

He wondered if he should apologize for being insensitive earlier or let that go. She had pegged him so accurately on his relationships that he wondered if his competitive nature had gotten the best of him. A "one-up-'em" type of mentality that he and his brother had played throughout their childhood and even still did sometimes as adults.

Trey knew that wasn't the case, though. He had really wanted to express that he understood that her pain was even deeper than being betrayed by Franklin. She had lost trust in someone and almost been killed in the process, but the fact that she had lost something as precious as a baby had to have been the worst part of her experience.

His sister-in-law's face flashed through his mind as he recalled her and his brother's pain when they lost their baby during her second pregnancy. Shelly had been five months along. They had been thankful to be able to at least hold their little girl and say goodbye.

Unfortunately, he had a habit of being too abrupt and not taking into consideration how someone might be affected. Another strike against him in his attempt for a long-term relationship.

Sandra abruptly removed her feet from the railing causing Trey instantly to be on alert. She placed her cereal bowl next to her coffee on the small table and stood. He pushed away from the column automatically placing his hand on his holstered gun while reaching for her arm. She jumped when he touched her, but didn't acknowledge him.

He followed her gaze and discovered what had caught her attention. An elderly gentleman was shuffling down the sidewalk across the street. He was bent slightly forward and appeared to be in his eighties. A tweed cap was perched on his head and he wore a dark windbreaker and slacks. Visible below the cap was thick, shocking white hair. Not many men of that age could brag about having that much hair. Although there was a promise of another warm spring day, he was swinging an umbrella tapping it on the sidewalk with every other step.

"Hello, Mr. Ferguson." Sandra gave him a brilliant smile. Trey released his hand from her arm.

Mr. Ferguson glanced up without missing a beat, stopped, tipped his hat and smiled at Sandra. "Good morning to you, Miss Johnson. There's another brilliant day blossoming."

"Yes, there is. I hope you have big plans."

"I may have to fiddle around in the yard and get my daily dose of vitamin D."

"You do that, it'll be good for you."

"Have a good day."

"Thank you, I will."

Mr. Ferguson returned to his walk making his way past two more houses before turning up the sidewalk of the third one. Sandra waited for him to safely make it into his house before turning and gathering her things. She walked past Trey and into the house without acknowledging him. Trey's day was going to be a long one.

———

DANNY EMERGED from the bathroom as they entered. The jeans

and long-sleeved T-shirt he was in seemed more his style. Sandra was glad to see the suit gone.

"Did you sleep okay?'"

"Yeah. Your couch was really comfortable." Danny headed into the kitchen and came back shortly with coffee.

"Aren't you going to eat?"

"Maybe later. I'm not much of a breakfast eater."

He took a sip of his coffee. From the pained expression on his face, Sandra guessed he must have taken too much and had burned the taste buds right off his tongue.

"So Sandra, what do we do today?"

"The same thing you saw yesterday. I have a number of clients coming to work out, a couple of massages and a nutritional consultation. You'll also have a chance to meet my part-time receptionist." Sandra tilted her head. "Actually, I think you might like her."

"We are not here for hook ups."

Trey stood in what Sandra had decided was his usual stance. He was leaning against the doorjamb of the kitchen, his arms folded across his chest. Like Danny, he was in jeans and wore a black T-shirt that emphasized his physique, something Sandra would have preferred not to think about. She had to remember she was still mad at him for bringing up the loss of the baby. He had had no right to be that personal with her.

Turning back to Danny she gave him a big smile and a wink. "I think you might hit it off. She's about your age, gorgeous and a great sense of humor."

"That's code for "she's a dog", Logan."

"She is not a "dog"." Sandra turned and glared at Trey. Some things never changed. The man was exasperating. "Danny, ignore Grumpy."

"Regardless of her appearance, we are not here to socialize, Ms. Johnson. We are here to do a job and then leave."

"What happened to calling me Sandra?" His stick-in-the-mud routine made it easy for Sandra to push his buttons.

"What does that mean?" He tilted his head with scowl in place.

"Last night, in my bedroom, you called me Sandra."

Chapter 7

Danny's head pivoted quickly between the two, his eyes huge with questions. Sandra turned her eyes to Trey as well hoping her face reflected the innocence she tried to feign.

Straightening from his position at the doorjamb, Sandra noted that the frown embedded in Trey's forehead had deepened and she wondered, for a moment, if she had gone too far.

"Don't go leading Logan on to believe something happened between us last night."

"Well, you did come into my bedroom, didn't you?" Again, the voice of innocence.

"Yeah, but...."

"And you did hold me, right?"

She felt a little bad for leading Danny into believing something had happened when nothing had, but at the same time she liked the fact that Trey might be squirming.

"Logan, she's deliberately leaving out details."

She raised an eyebrow at Danny.

"Damn it, Logan, she's a woman. She'd embellish any story."

"So you're saying I haven't told Danny the truth?"

Trey's irritation was quite obvious and she wondered if she

should give Danny the complete story before Trey exploded or had a brain aneurysm.

"No. Nothing you've said is false." A wicked smile appeared and the frown disappeared. "However you left out the part about how you clung to me until you stopped moaning."

Oh my, Lord. He had one-upped her. It was all she could do not to burst out laughing. "Yes, you're right. I did leave that part out."

Poor Danny was still puzzled, but the bantering had put a smile on Trey's face. This wasn't the first time she had wondered why he didn't smile more. The transformation was remarkable and he almost seemed human.

When they arrived at Sandra's business, Danny stayed outside with her while Trey checked the interior. The man of few words was back in business mode and motioned them in when he was done. Sandra started the day in her office where she took time to go over the schedule and make sure she had everything ready for the day's business.

She checked the messages as she sat in her chair. The first one was from Mary Howard who was canceling her appointment because one of her kids was sick. The second message had her calling out for Trey. Her tone of voice had him in there in no time.

"What is it?"

"Listen to this."

Danny joined them as Trey leaned on her desk. She played back the message.

"Have you missed me, Sandra? I've missed you."

There was no doubt the caller was Mark and he chuckled as if he found the situation amusing. "I promised I would come for you, remember? No matter what you do or where you are, I will find you. I thought I'd surprise you, but decided it would be more fun knowing you were scared because you won't ever know when I'm coming."

By the time the messaged ended, Trey had taken up position in the office doorway, presumably to scan the street. He then motioned Danny to station himself at the front door.

Trey returned to Sandra's desk. "This should re-emphasize how important it is that you never to go anywhere without Logan or me by your side. Don't walk out the front door of your house or business or take off in your car without one of us. If we're lucky, this will be over in the next twenty-four hours and he won't have even crossed the county line. Until then, you need to follow our instructions. Is that clear?"

She nodded her head since words refused to come out of her mouth. Sandra understood too well. The phone message had brought the dream from the night before racing to the forefront reminding her how too real the situation had become.

She knew the blood had drained from her face at the shock that Mark Franklin once again had invaded her personal space. As much as she would have liked to forget the phone call, the fears the dream had elicited still coursed through her body.

The sense of doom and destruction had felt real after the nightmare. This morning, in the light of day, she thought she had put the dream into perspective. The sense of terror, though, was lurking below the surface and could emerge at any time. Sandra now feared her dream was a premonition. She shuddered at the thought.

Anxiety and panic attacks had been the demons that had lived with her for months after the attempt on her life. Thankfully, with good counseling and some help with anti-anxiety drugs, she had come out healthy on the other side.

With Mark behind bars and her treatments for the physical, mental and emotional injuries completed, she had uprooted and moved to a new town to start over. Close enough to family, but far enough away from the memories of her personal hell. Now she could feel the same hell closing in on her as if it were yesterday.

When Trey and Danny had shown up the day before, there had been a tinge of that anxiety. She had ignored the sign. She had breathed through it. The dream had brought on an anxiety attack, but she had fought back, forbidding her body to succumb. Now, she didn't know. She could feel the anxiety start in the pit of her stomach with its brother panic not far away.

The fact that revenge could be such a driving force for someone was beyond her comprehension. She would never have thought the man who had once been her fiancée could have turned into such a monster. It was as if Mark had lost the gene for compassion and understanding.

"I understand. Believe me I understand."

Sandra headed out to the workout area, pushing past Trey. She needed space. Her office had suddenly become too small and she felt as though she were suffocating. She needed air to breathe.

Sandra stopped in front of the standing fan running in the corner of the room. The air felt good on her overheated skin. The cool breeze helped clear her head of the "what ifs". She stayed there for several minutes with her eyes closed and did the slow breathing her counselor had taught her for such an event as this. She let the past pain float away. When she finally felt she could face the world again, she opened her eyes and took one more deep breath.

Trey and Danny waited patiently at their respective posts. Danny fidgeted with the pen he held in his hand. As usual, she couldn't read Trey, who was lounging against the door of her office, arms crossed. She would never have guessed he could be so patient. But then again, he had surprised her in the last twenty-four hours.

"Sandra, we will do everything in our power to see that no harm comes to you. We are the best at what we do."

His comment was delivered without his usual business attitude and softened by the use of her first name. Trey's reassurance gave her something to hold onto until Mark was once again behind bars. For the second time in less then ten hours, Trey Walker had shown her he was human. There was hope yet.

"Okay, I'm done feeling sorry for myself and I still have a business to run." She walked towards Trey and clapped her hands. "Out of my way."

He obediently stepped to one side so she could enter her office.

———————

TREY FIXED the back door while Danny continued with his post at the front door. And Sandra spent the next few hours paying bills and working with a couple of clients.

Trey replaced the temporary fix from the night before with two deadbolts. If someone wanted to get in that way, they were going to have to take an axe to the door.

Logan helped him with the setting of the bolts and Trey was surprised at how natural he seemed to be at fixing things. In view of how fast he could destroy most things, Trey had expected him to be more in the way then actually contributing. Perhaps he would have to give Logan some slack. After all, being in the field was a far cry from his normal desk job.

The front door chime announced another arrival right before noon and, as Trey had done throughout the morning, he reached a hand to rest on the harnessed gun nestled at his lower back. To the casual observer, he appeared innocent enough, but Trey knew he could drop someone before the door closed behind them.

Expecting another client, he was caught off guard when the young woman who walked in looked like she had stepped out of a modeling shoot.

Her legs travelled on forever, emphasized by high heels and a short skirt that seemed to float and flutter around them. Although she was too young to interest him, he found it hard to take his eyes off her. Her long, dark hair seemed impossibly thick and was the kind of hair men dreamed of running their fingers through. He didn't think he could be any more entranced, but found he was wrong when she took her sunglasses off. Her big brown eyes were surrounded by long eyelashes and were lit up by the smile she gave Sandra.

Something hard pushed against Trey startling him out of the daze the girl had temporarily trapped him in. Logan had practically tripped over himself as he pushed past him to stare at the breath of fresh air talking to Sandra.

Logan had also become caught up by the enchantment of the young lady. He gaped at her, completely under the spell of a woman he had yet to meet.

Understanding fully what he was experiencing, Trey couldn't help, but feel sorry for him, knowing she was well beyond his reach. This was a woman who probably had men lined up around the block willing to outwait a current boyfriend in order to have an opportunity to spend even a moment with her.

Disgusted with himself for losing sight even for a brief moment why he was there, he took his frustration out on the person nearest to him.

"It's a girl, Logan. She's not the latest attraction at the zoo."

"Uh huh."

Sandra and the newcomer started walking toward them. Two complete opposites and yet equally beautiful and exciting.

Although Logan only had eyes for Sandra's friend, Trey found he couldn't take his eyes off Sandra.

When had he become so aware of her little nuances? Her nose crinkled a little when she smiled and a very small dimple appeared to the right of her lips. Although she hadn't yet treated him with that smile, he had noticed it when she interacted with her clients and Danny. He wanted to think that he had noticed so much about her because of his training, but he would only be fooling himself. Sandra's small dimple emphasized lips that needed to be kissed. They were inviting and his stomach clenched every time she licked them.

When he first met her, he had immediately been attracted to her, which had surprised and aggravated him at the same time. There was a spirit about her that spoke of her strength to fight and survive anything. He had been impressed at how she had handled the news about Franklin, even when he knew she would have liked to have been on the next train and run away.

Her nightmare, however, had shown her weakness. She had been at her most vulnerable clinging to him, no longer able to put up a brave front. The fact that he had enjoyed holding her in his arms had not been lost on him even if he had tried denying the feeling.

Now as she walked towards them, he found himself once again physically reacting to her. Once again he wondered if he had gone too long without a girlfriend. From the moment he had taken on his duties as a Marshal, he had never allowed himself to be attracted to anyone even remotely close to his work. Now he was going to have to figure out how to keep Sandra from being a distraction. The type of work he did wasn't conducive to interruptions. Distractions were dangerous to everyone you were in contact with.

"Guys, this Lacy. She's my receptionist."

Trey noticed how this last was directed at Logan. No wonder

Sandra had mentioned her this morning. She was right in believing Logan would be interested, but if she thought Lacy would ever be interested in Logan, she was going to be disappointed. Whereas Lacy was confident and beautiful, Logan acted as if he didn't know if he was coming or going. He was not a man someone would associate with Lacy. She was put together and he was a constant disaster.

"Lacy, this is Trey Walker and Danny Logan."

————

SHE EXTENDED her hand to each of them as Sandra introduced them.

"Danny, I gave Lacy a little background, but perhaps you would like to answer any additional questions she may have."

"Sure. Why don't we go over to your desk."

Trey watched a transformation come over Logan. He confidently took Lacy by the elbow and escorted her to the receptionist desk. Now that he was in charge, he had suddenly emerged from his cocoon and Lacy seemed to respond to him.

"I'll be damned."

"What?"

"Yesterday, he could barely walk and talk at the same time and managed to destroy everything in his path. Today he meets a beautiful woman and he does it effortlessly."

"Did you ever think he was a walking disaster because of you?"

He turned to Sandra. "Me? Why me?"

"Why not you? He was obviously nervous yesterday and every time you barked, he visibly jumped."

"I'm not responsible for how he reacts."

"Maybe not, but you are responsible for how you treat people which can determine how they react."

"Did you minor in psychology?"

"It's human nature, Walker. Sometimes you need to take responsibility for your actions, including how they affect others."

She turned and walked back to her office. He caught up with her before she walked around the desk. Taking her arm, he turned her to face him. The momentum brought her closer to him than he had intended. The smell of her perfume made his stomach warm. She was flesh and blood and close. He had to overcome the sudden urge to kiss her.

"And how do I affect you, Sandra Johnson?"

Trey had meant to continue their conversation about Logan when he had followed her. Instead he had done the unthinkable and asked a personal question not related to the job at hand. The question had come out as a suggestive whisper. Somewhere between the workroom and her office, his professional side had been kicked to a corner of his mind. His subconscious had taken over when he touched her. The subconscious that was attracted to her as a man is suppose to be to a woman. No longer being of sound mind, he hadn't been able to stop the question from spilling out.

He became fascinated as the pulse at the base of her neck quickened. He heard her breath become shallow and fast. Her lips parted and she licked them, whether in anticipation or in trying to form an answer, he didn't know. The action hit him in the gut and it took all his will power not to pull her to him and test the softness of her lips.

"You have no effect on me, Walker."

He realized too late that he had paid too much attention to the movement of her lips as she answered and his desire sent him over the edge.

"Liar. " He touched the pulse at the base of her throat with his thumb to prove his point and then slowly dropped his head towards her giving her ample warning of his intentions. If she had any objections, she didn't voice them.

He never took his eyes from hers as he continued on what he knew would be a path of self-destruction. She closed her eyes when their lips were, but a breath-width apart. He finally closed his and took what she offered.

Over these past years, he had never veered from the focus of the job at hand. This was a dangerous route to take. This path he was taking could leave an agent vulnerable and open to mistakes. Mistakes that could prove deadly for both the agent and client.

As he deepened the kiss and pulled Sandra closer, his mind started registering the implications of his actions and he knew he needed to stop while he still had his sanity.

For a moment longer, though, he gave himself permission to feel her fit body against his, relishing the softness of her breasts pressed to his chest. He nipped at her lower lip and when her lips parted, he took the opportunity to delve into the warm moistness that tasted of coffee and pure bliss. The kiss was an experience itself. An experience Trey wanted to indulge in over and over again.

Voices from the other room broke through the haze that had engulfed his better judgment. He eased himself from Sandra, taking a few steps away from her for some much-needed breathing space right before Logan stepped through the door. Both of them were breathing fast. Sandra's face was flushed, the desire in her eyes slowly fading.

"Hey, Boss, I've finished catching Lacy up on our assignment. What's next on the agenda?"

———

SANDRA WAS HAVING problems clearing her head. The wires

seemed to be mismatched and she was having trouble making sense of what had just happened. How could she have let him past her defenses? When had her common sense run away? Even after Danny entered the room, she didn't take her eyes off Trey for several seconds. When she finally did, the enchantment he had cast was slow to dissolve. The spell was like the groggy feeling you have when trying to wake after taking a sleeping pill.

"Now, we hang out, Logan, and hope we receive a phone call soon letting us know they've picked up Franklin."

Sandra glanced at Trey and saw he had his game face on again, his eyes still locked on her. His comment made it perfectly clear he was ready for the task of babysitting her to be over. What was she expecting? The job would end when Mark was caught. That was a given when they had shown up. The kiss hadn't changed anything. The kiss had simply been two adults acting on the attraction they felt for each other.

So why did she feel betrayed? She knew why. She had allowed another man under her skin for a fraction of a second. She let him make her feel something again and that had left her vulnerable. She had given him permission to step through the small gap she had left open to the possibility of a connection. He had only done what she had invited him to do

"Okay, I'll be in front then and will keep an eye out."

"Logan."

"Yeah?"

"Remember, you are here to do a job, not to hook up with the receptionist."

So that was that, Sandra thought. He had forgotten his job for a brief moment and he was reminding himself as well as her why he was here. That was fine. The kiss had been a kiss. Just a kiss. A brief distraction where she hadn't thought about Mark Franklin and the danger he presented.

The kiss had also been a reminder of how she needed to

continue to be vigilant as to whom she gave her kisses as well as her heart. That had been a painful lesson learned from Mark and she wasn't willing to go that course again.

What she wasn't willing to examine quite yet was how, of all people, she had decided to allow Trey through the barriers she had so carefully erected around herself. She decided to ignore those thoughts for now. They weren't worth examining since he would be gone in a matter of days, if not hours.

"If you guys will excuse me, I have some work that needs to be done."

The feeling of being under Trey's spell had faded. Remnants still lingered, but give her a few hours and even those would be gone. The barriers would be solidly back in place and life would go on as she had planned.

Chapter 8

Mark could feel the sweat break out on the back of his neck, belying the outward calm he presented. He was stuck in traffic, backed up on a small four-lane highway. Up ahead he could make out several flashing lights belonging to police cars. Either there was a terrible accident or this was a police barricade. He hoped for an accident. If it wasn't an accident, which meant they were searching for someone and the chances were that they were looking for him.

The line of cars was creeping forward, slowly putting him closer to the police activity. Mark could make out one officer motioning cars on past them. The car he was in he had taken from a business parking lot that morning. He had figured he would have until the end of the workday before the owner would report the car missing. But he was starting to think his luck had run out. Other cars had him pinned in as they jockeyed for position to form one lane. There wasn't an escape route to be found. Cars on one side and a concrete barrier on the other.

As he came within a dozen cars of the activity, he was finally close enough to see that it was an accident. At the same time, an ambulance pulled up to the scene with another one off in the distance. Mark breathed a sigh of relief. He still had time.

He took off his ball cap for a second and used his T-shirt sleeve to wipe the moisture from his forehead.

Not wanting to take any chances on being recognized, he put the cap back on and pulled it low to his eyes. With sunglasses and a hat on, there wasn't anything distinct about him that should give him away. He was still hoping news of his escape hadn't reached this far. By taking a route authorities might overlook, he had hoped to save a lot of trouble. Having this many cops in the vicinity, though, was making him itch to put as much distance between them and him as quickly as possible.

Relief was fleeting when the cop motioned it was his turn to pass the accident, only to be stopped as the second ambulance came on the scene. When Mark thought the officer was ready to let him through again, he instead motioned for him to roll down his window as he walked towards him. Mark's instinct was to floor the gas pedal, but he managed to keep his cool and did as the officer asked.

"Yes, officer?" Mark graced him with the smile that had charmed so many of clients.

"You have a headlight out. Thought you might want to take care of that before you're pulled over for it."

"I had no idea. Thanks. I appreciate that." Relief hummed through his body.

"Have a nice day." The officer motioned for him to move on.

"You, too."

Mark refrained from pushing hard on the gas pedal, instead following the example of the previous cars, taking his time to ease past the accident before he took the car to cruising speed.

That had been too close. He questioned whether going after Sandra was really such a good idea. It would be so much easier to cruise on down into Mexico and hook up with his pen pal.

But then he remembered the past few years he had spent in jail because of her, and the slow burn of revenge once again invaded his soul. She was going to have to suffer for what she had put him through. He needed to finish what he had started.

He took the next exit that advertised a parts store. Pulling into the parking lot, he took a second to acquaint himself with the area in case he had to leave quickly.

Once in the store, he headed to the display for headlights. There were a few locals hanging out at the counter discussing the upcoming crop season, a TV on in the background and a customer being rung up. Mark found what he wanted and started towards the register to pay. He stopped in his tracks when he saw his face plastered across the television screen. Everyone at the counter had stopped talking to watch the breaking news report of an escaped convict.

"Mark Franklin walked away from the prison after subduing the jail officer who was making final rounds. He left disguised as that jail officer, walking past the rest of the employees as the shift ended. The officer's car was found sixty miles away in the town of Rockville, where leads have dried up. Authorities believe his ultimate goal is Mexico, but would like to reach him before then. Meanwhile, a lot of questions are still unanswered starting with how an inmate could subdue a jail officer without arousing the attention of the rest of the prison. Are our prison systems really as secure as they want us to believe?"

The door closed behind Mark as the news piece started to explore the prison system. He was leaving while the other customers were occupied with the story. For the second time in an hour, he managed to temper the urgency to leave in a hurry. He hadn't traveled this far to have stupidity take him down. Since there was plenty of daylight left, he kept the headlights off until he came to a place that would be safe for him to change the light that was out without being surrounded by people.

At least they hadn't figured out where he had gone since Rockville. They were probably still trying to search for information from the bus station. Even if they did figure out that "Joe McIntyre" was Mark Franklin, they would have to take time to check each bus stop. He could only hope they would concentrate first on the far side of the state where his ticket was supposed to have taken him.

———

"WALKER, you have to do something with him. I'm not going to have a business left to run if he destroys anything else. Not to mention, I don't think my insurance covers puppy love."

Sandra regarded the latest disaster. In Danny's attempt to help Lacy, he had forgotten to turn off the water to the utility sink. Thank God she had walked back just seconds after the water started overflowing. Of course, the only reason she had come back to the room was for some rags to wipe off the massage oil he had left on some weights after touching them. *What was it with Danny and massage oil?*

"Hey, you're the one that wanted him to become acquainted with Lacy. What did you expect? I told you not to play matchmaker."

"Jump off your high horse, Walker. Have you thought that if you actually tried to teach him something we might all benefit?"

"He won't be with me that long."

"My point exactly. You seem only interested in how this affects you and could care less how it affects the rest of us. It's not like you don't have the time to give him some direction. Isn't the whole purpose of this assignment to help both of you understand how the other party functions?"

"It's a waste of time with him. He's an experiment in the office. After this session, he probably won't be sent out again."

"And here I thought you cared about your job and took it seriously."

Sandra threw towels on the floor and started mopping up the remnants of water that hadn't made it to the floor drain. Standing, she threw the towels into the now empty sink. Turning to grab some more towels, she was surprised to find Trey helping.

"You don't have to do that."

"As you pointed out, I have lots of time."

"So go spend that time with Danny. Give him something other than your exasperated sighs and frowns. Give him some encouragement. Make him feel like he's worthy."

Trey stood from his crouching position, frowning.

"Didn't your mother ever tell you your face would freeze in that position if you did that too often? Or is that too late?"

"Didn't your mother ever tell you if you can't say something nice, don't say anything at all?"

"She did, but she hadn't met you."

He ran a hand threw his hair and threw the wet towel into the sink. "So you think I should talk to him?"

Sandra clasped her hands together in begging form. "Yes, please, stop this madness before I commit myself to the psych ward. Give him some of your time."

"Fine. I'll give him a little of my time. But you may owe me before this is over."

"I'll make you a nice homemade meal tonight."

"You would have done that anyway."

"Yes, but I promise I won't spit in it."

He mumbled something Sandra was glad she couldn't hear as he left the room. Now maybe things would settle down so she could finish some work.

———

"Logan, how can you be so smart when with the computer stuff and not have a clue about human nature?"

Trey had been with him less then fifteen minutes and was ready to follow Sandra to the psych ward. He noticed he had been checking his phone every few minutes since sitting down with Logan. He was sure he must have missed the phone call telling him this assignment was over.

"I guess I'm more comfortable with computers."

"You can be both. Hell, when you met Lacy, you did a great job of shedding your geekiness. How did you do that?"

Logan observed the subject in question. "I don't know, except she didn't make me feel uncomfortable. I'm use to having people pigeon hole me and she took me at face value."

Trey thought about Logan's answer and felt guilty that he hadn't taken Logan at face value. He had a habit of immediately placing people in a category when he met them. Logan had been no exception.

"I gather you've had that happen more than once?"

"Yeah. Most of the time I do really well, but I can always feel a vibe when I know someone doesn't want to be around me."

"I gather I've given you that vibe."

Logan nodded in response. "My Dad wasn't really part of my growing up years and when he did show up, he made it clear he wasn't pleased with how I turned out."

"What could he possibly be unhappy about? Good education, good job, smart kid."

Logan glanced at the floor. "Because my job is behind a desk and not out in the field like a "real Marshal"."

Logan's comment made it clear that his dad and Trey ranked in the same category. This was a book smart kid fresh out of college making his way in the world and now, Trey realized, had more on the ball than either he or his absent father had given him credit for. Trey did believe his job in the field was more important. He had never given recognition to others in the department who were essential in every case a Field Marshal took on.

"Yeah. That's rough." Trey sighed wondering how he could apologize without feeling foolish. "Too many of us do that, I'm afraid. We have a bad habit of judging a book by its cover. The truth is, we couldn't do our job if you guys weren't behind the scenes feeding us the information we need." Trey once again ran a hand through his hair this time frustrated with himself.

"Let's start over. You have accomplished more than most people will in a lifetime. Hold that close to your vest and don't let others determine how you feel about yourself. Including me."

Logan visibly relaxed. "I honestly do want to know how you do your job and what I can take back to my work that will benefit the agency."

"Deal." Trey held out his hand and Logan accepted the truce.

———

SANDRA WALKED out of her office just then and couldn't stop from smiling when she saw them. She hoped that meant her house and business would once again be safe from ruin.

"Lacy, I need to run this stuff to the bank. Can you hold down the fort for a few minutes?"

"Not a problem."

She grabbed her purse and the deposit envelope and headed to the front door. As Sandra reached to push the door open, Trey stepped in front of her and her hand ended up planted on his broad chest. Sandra pulled her hand back quickly, but not before his warmth had seeped into her fingers giving her goose bumps.

"Did you forget the rules?"

"Rules? Oh, the rules." She rolled her eyes.

"Yeah. I escort you wherever you go. Exciting, huh?"

"Beyond my wildest dreams."

Sandra waved her hand for him to go ahead of her. Trey walked out, scanning the area before letting her follow. She thanked him for holding the door as she walked past.

"Your attitude seems to have improved, Johnson."

"You bring out the best in me, I guess."

"I'd hate to see what your worst is."

Sandra squinted against the brightness of the day. His lips were slightly curved in what she assumed was a smile. His sunglasses kept her from reading his eyes.

"Are you trying your hand at humor now, Walker? If so, I'd stick to your day job."

His smile grew bigger. "So you think I'm at least good at that, huh?"

"You have your moments. Did you and Danny at least make some progress?"

"We'll see."

They paused at the intersection, waiting for the light to turn. She noted how Trey never let his eyes linger on any one area. Even behind his shades, she knew his eyes were watching everything and everyone around them.

"This would have been much safer if we had driven."

"I'm not going to drive two blocks and waste the gas. Besides, this way you can actually earn your money."

"Believe me, with what I've already had to endure between you and Logan, I should be paid combat pay."

"Why me? I haven't physically assaulted you."

"Your damn dog."

"You're still holding a grudge about that? You've seen how sweet he is."

"He could eat someone with one bite."

"Tiny's a pussycat." Sandra paused. "Wait. You're really scared of dogs?"

"No."

"Come on, Walker, fess up. They scare you."

"I don't see the point in having one."

"Wow. Big, brave Walker has a kryptonite. Who would have thought."

She knew he was irritated with the direction of the conversation. On the other hand, she couldn't keep the smile from her face.

"Here we are."

Trey did his thing again, glancing around before going ahead of Sandra into the bank and scanning the area quickly.

The last twenty-four hours seemed like a television drama gone badly downhill. She hoped Trey's phone would ring soon. Heaven knew she had been willing the damn thing to do so since the Marshals walked in her door. She wanted to be able to go somewhere without feeling like she was attached to someone. The situation put a whole new meaning on the term "smother" in a relationship.

"Could you at least take your sunglasses off? You look like my bodyguard."

"I am."

"Maybe so, but I'd prefer not to advertise it."

Trey removed his glasses, slipping them onto the neckline of his T-shirt. Their weight pulled the shirt down giving Sandra a glimpse of the pulse at the base of his neck. His pulse was steady and sure, not at all like hers that had taken off at a trot. Just remembering the few times she had come into direct contact with him made her a little light-headed. The thought of repeating a kiss with him caused a whirl of butterflies in her stomach. Her thoughts were abruptly interrupted when he motioned for her that it was her turn at the teller.

"Hey, Margo," Sandra greeted the teller who was eyeing Trey.

"Hey, Sandra. Anything new going on?"

Margo opened the deposit bag and pulled bills and checks out to count. Her eyes flickered to Trey off and on as he watched everything around him, not noticing the effect he was having on the tellers, including Frank at the drive-thru.

"No, everything is the same."

Margo lifted an eyebrow and tilted her head towards Trey. "So is he a figment of your imagination that has filtered its way into mine?"

"Funny. No this is a... a.... my cousin from out of town. Visiting." Trey turned around as he realized he was the subject of their conversation. "Trey, this is Margo," Sandra said, introducing them.

"Nice to meet you." Trey didn't blink an eye at the exclamation Sandra gave.

"A cousin, huh? Sandra never mentioned she had such good family genes." Margo smiled at Trey.

"Oh, these aren't the good genes. You haven't met my Dad's side of the family." Sandra watched as one of Trey's eyebrows rose. "Now there are some good genes, if you know what I mean."

"She's right. Sandra's Dad's side is much better looking. She and I ended up with her Mom's side."

Sandra couldn't help but burst out laughing. "Touché".

"EVERYONE GET YOUR HANDS UP WHERE I CAN SEE THEM!"

Chapter 9

All eyes turned to the front door. A slightly built man with a ski mask over his face waved a handgun back and forth. Sandra knew Trey had his gun safely tucked in the back of his pants, but he didn't try to retrieve it. The jacket he had thrown on before leaving Sandra's gym hid the weapon.

He slowly raised his hands nodding to Sandra to follow suit. Others throughout the bank were doing the same thing, stunned by the scene unfolding before them. She wasn't sure what Trey's plan was, but she knew he had one. His attention was once again on the gunman. This probably wasn't going to end well for the masked man.

Trey had managed to edge himself closer to Sandra, blocking her from the gunman. "Is that Franklin?" He whispered.

"No. Mark is much taller and has wide shoulders."

The thought hadn't even crossed her mind that this could have been Mark. Considering the frame of mind he had been in when he tried running her over and again when he managed to break out of prison, she should have realized he was capable of doing something as crazy as robbing a bank. The implication made her knees shake as adrenaline raced through her veins. For the second time in several hours, she was reminded of how much her life was truly in danger.

The man swinging his gun at them could have been Mark, and if he had been, she knew without a doubt that he would have killed her in front of everyone.

"Everyone on the floor except the tellers. I still want to see your hands."

The whole process seemed to unfold in slow motion as the customers lowered themselves first to their knees and then flat on the ground. Sandra noted that Trey had managed to edge himself closer to the gunman, before lowering himself to the ground. That also meant he was further away from her and panic started to set in. She did her best to calm the erratic beat of her heart, practicing her slow breathing and concentrating on the rhythm. She could hear someone on the other side of the room crying softly and she remembered seeing old Mrs. Tanner in the bank. Sandra wondered if she was the one upset.

"Who has a key to the doors? Get over here and lock them."

Sandra peeked and saw Carlee head to the doors.

"Now your turn, get on the floor." He turned the gun back to the other tellers. "You and you, come out here and do the same."

Frank and Stacey did as they were told, leaving only Margo behind the counter.

"Okay, you start getting some money together. None of those dye packets either or I'll come back for you."

Sandra could hear drawers being opened behind her. The gunman started walking to the counter to retrieve his goody bag. Sandra caught Trey's movement and watched as he rolled once towards the gunman and kicked the legs out from under him. A loud shot echoed as the gunman fell, causing Sandra to flinch and leaving her ears ringing. Before the gunman could do anything, Trey was on his feet with his own gun pressed against the man's forehead.

"Let go of the gun." As the gunman released his weapon, Trey kicked it a short distance away. "Now on your belly and spread your arms and legs. Someone call the police. Sandra, make sure that stray bullet didn't hit anyone. Everyone else, just stay calm until the police arrive."

Trey pulled the robber's mask off and there was an audible gasp in the room.

"Jimmy Jones!" Mrs. Tanner scolded. She was a dominant force even at five feet tall and barely a hundred pounds. Her hands were fisted and resting on her hips, a pinch of disgust etched on her face. "Young man, your mama is not going to be pleased with this latest stunt. She brought you up better than that."

Sandra moved to help Mrs. Tanner settle in a comfortable chair and got some water for her. The woman had to be in her mid-eighties and nothing seemed to faze her. There were no traces of tears on her face that meant she had not been the one who had been crying.

The police arrived quickly. After several minutes of explaining what had happened, Trey joined Sandra.

"It'll take a while before we can leave. They need statements from everyone."

"Nice work, Walker. Where'd you learn that leg move? Marshal training?"

"No, that was courtesy of wrestling with my brothers."

"You have brothers?"

"Two."

"You must have driven your Mom crazy."

"Only when we broke stuff."

Sandra chuckled. The thought of Trey as a rambunctious

child, playing like a real boy, didn't match the image she had of him.

"Why's that funny?"

"It's hard for me to imagine that you knew how to have fun at one point in your life."

"I know how to have fun now."

"No, Walker, I don't think you do."

"You've only seen me working."

"True. That's why I have trouble picturing you relaxing and enjoying the moment you're in. You are such a by-the-book-guy it's hard to imagine your personal life is any different. Everything in its place and all that."

"There's nothing wrong with being orderly."

"So I'm right?"

He only glared at her, not wanting to acknowledge she had hit the nail on the head. Fortunately he didn't have to answer since it was her turn for a statement.

———

WATCHING the movement and expressions of her face as she responded to police questions had him wondering, not for the first time, why she drove him crazy. As things were, Logan was turning out to be the least of his worries. Sandra had become a thorn in his side. She antagonized him on purpose. He wasn't sure if that was because of him or the circumstances or both. Certainly he wouldn't be here if it weren't for Mark Franklin's escape from jail. .

Trey rubbed his chest trying to erase the small twinge that had occurred at the thought. No one he had ever met kept him guessing like she did. She was incredibly compassionate with her clients, as well as with Logan. The patience she exhibited with each client amazed him. Every one of them had something to complain about, from husbands not listening, to nosy neighbors, to complaints about their weight. Sandra seemed to take everything in stride. She listened and didn't miss a beat with the right words of support and concern.

When she dealt with him, however, she seemed to be on a mission to needle him. Their conversations were laced with sarcasm. Trey realized he wanted more from her. He wanted what her clients and Logan had with her. He wanted her compassion. He wanted her full attention. He wanted her to care.

God, where did those thoughts come from?

He rose abruptly and walked a short distance away deciding that he needed to stretch his legs. What hex had she put on him that he worried whether or not she cared about him? The last thing he needed in his life was someone who drove him crazy. He glanced back at her as she stood and shook hands with the policeman. She drove him insane, and yet he was drawn to her more than he cared to admit.

Work must be wearing him down. He hadn't taken any time off for a while. That's probably what he needed. He decided right then and there that when this case was over he was taking a vacation.

———

"Okay, boys, here we are."

They entered an upscale bar where Sandra met with her friends once every two months. As much as Trey had tried to convince her that she should skip this month's gathering, she refused to succumb to his bullying. Ever since the bank robbery, he had seemed exceptionally surly, which only made Sandra dig her feet in deeper refusing to budge because he said she should. She needed to regroup and catch up with friends she hadn't seen since the month before. Each of them were busy with their lives and, with the exception of those who used her as a trainer, this was sometimes their only way to keep connected. This was a night to celebrate friendship.

She knew her friends well. They were single, and most of them were big flirts. There would be no mercy shown towards Trey tonight when they set their eyes on him. He'd be trapped. She knew it wasn't very nice of her to throw him to the sharks, but she had this perverted need to watch him squirm. Tonight she had asked Lacy to join them for Danny's sake. One more little item guaranteed to irritate Trey.

He hadn't been happy when she had announced she was meeting friends. His frown had deepened when he couldn't convince her to stay in for the night. The fact that his forehead had remained in the same position since, kept a slight smile on her face and an extra bounce to her step.

She wasn't really sure why she took pleasure in tormenting him. Perhaps she wanted to see how far she could push him. Or perhaps doing so took her mind off why he was there.

His disbelief when they entered the bar added to her enjoyment and he didn't even know the half of what was yet to come.

"We can't stay here."

"Why not?"

"It's a bar."

"Yeah, that's kind of the point. In case you've completely lost touch with society, Walker, this is where one comes to drink and to even get drunk."

She smiled at him and he glared back.

"My point is that being here makes it harder to protect you. There's no place to really position ourselves and watch everyone coming and going."

"I guess that's your problem. By the way, since you're driving, I'm going to drink."

He had no choice but to follow, with Logan trailing, as they wound their way between the tables and chairs. Sandra greeted acquaintances as they passed groups of people until she stopped at a large booth filled with three women, including Lacy, and Frank.

"Hey guys. I hope you don't mind, but I brought some new blood."

"Mm, the eye candy you brought to the bank this morning." Frank raised an eyebrow and his martini glass. "There's always room for more. Pull up some chairs."

Sandra squeezed into the booth as Trey and Danny pulled up chairs. Trey positioned himself at the opposite end of the booth from Sandra, while Danny placed his chair next to her.

She watched Trey case the area and carefully look over the clientele. His location gave him the easiest access for watching whoever came through the front door. The only things behind him were the restrooms and back door that were Danny's responsibilities.

Sandra knew she might regret pushing Trey this far, but on the other hand, she refused to put her life on hold for a situation she didn't ask to be in.

She had chosen not to share the real reason why Trey and Danny were with her. Only a few knew about her past. Introducing them as cousins, instead, had been easier. Trey didn't have much choice but to let them know he was a Marshal since most of the north side of town would have found out after the attempted bank robbery.

After introductions were made, Sandra sat back, catching up with the latest news and gossip. Frank regaled them with the story of Jimmy Jones trying to rob the bank. In his glory of story-telling, Frank elaborated on the heroic deed Trey had performed saving them from sure harm.

Trey leaned back in his chair, legs extended and crossed at

the ankles. He was no longer frowning and appeared relaxed, except for the occasional tick at the corner of his right eye. Sandra was sure she was the only one aware of the twitch.

An hour into the reunion, Sandra was well into her second drink and realized she should have had more to eat than the banana she had grabbed before coming. Oh, well, she wasn't driving and it had been a while since she had given herself permission to drink enough to enjoy a buzz. Feeling more relaxed than she had since Trey showed up, she decided to enjoy the evening with abandon.

Her attention returned time and again to Trey, watching as he entertained the table with stories of his work. He stuck to stories along the line of what had happened at the bank that day. Ones, that ended well with no blood and guts.

Sandra couldn't help but smile at Frank as he stared at Trey, seemingly mesmerized by his splendor. Once in a while he would sigh and take a slow sip of his drink. He was obviously infatuated. Frank was easily on his third dirty martini and she knew when it was time to leave, they may well have to catch him when he stood up. Sandra made a mental note that someone would need to drive him home tonight.

Danny was totally relaxed and in heaven. Not only did he have the attention of Lacy, but most of the other women, all of who had been kind enough to listen to him and do a little flirting. If he had been a peacock, each one of his plumes would have been spread in an elaborate headdress with fabulous colors. Sandra noted that Danny managed all of this and still do his job. Like Trey, he was very aware of what was going on around him. She was very proud of him.

Sandra was impressed with how Trey had held up under the bombardment of female attention. He always seemed uptight, so seeing him relax as much as he could while working had surprised her. But there was no doubt he was still on the job. No one else seemed to notice his slight movements while surveying the bar.

Tami, one of her closes friends and the biggest flirt, sat right next to Trey, making a point to touch him often as she talked to him. As the evening progressed, she draped one arm over his shoulder and used her perfectly manicured fingernails of her other hand to graze his forearm. She was close enough to be able to whisper in his ear, which she did time and time again.

What surprised Sandra was that Trey flirted back and, by all appearances, seemed to be quite taken with her. Not that she could fault him. After all, Tami was stunning. She had short black hair and the biggest blue eyes, surrounded by the longest, natural eyelashes Sandra had ever seen. Most guys couldn't help but fall into the abyss of her soul when they saw those eyes.

Somewhere in the recesses of her buzzed-state of mind, the scene before her started becoming annoying. Trey was giving his attention to Tami, yet he could barely be civil to her, let alone share a smile the way he seemed to do so easily with Tami.

There was the one time he had let his guard down and had given Sandra a genuine smile. She remembered her physical response to that smile. Her body had ignited with heat and her heart had started racing. It had only been for a moment, but boy, what a moment. Since then he had gone back to his pain-in-the-ass ways. She didn't know why she bothered with him.

Sandra sighed. It must be her. He wasn't having issues sharing his smile with everyone else at the table. Trey was leaning towards Tami as she whispered some tidbit in his ear making him laugh. Her manicured hand lay on his arm possessively and her silicone breasts were pressed up against him. Overcome by a sudden urge to rip her friend's eyes out, Sandra took a large swig of her drink.

Thoughts of maiming her friend flew out of her head when Trey's attention suddenly turned to her. As he made eye contact with her, everyone else at the table faded away. He gave her a slow and seductive smile, causing heat to spread throughout her limbs leaving her fingers and lips numb with the desire to touch and taste him.

His smile made her feel like the sexiest woman in the room. The only woman in the room. Her eyes drifted to his lips, wanting to feel them again. Bravado washed through her, encouraged by the drink in her hand. She could be appalled later when the alcohol had left her system and her brain neurons were connected again.

Her eyes drifted back to his and she was thankful she was already sitting for her legs would have given out. She wasn't mistaken this time. Desire smoldered in his eyes and it wasn't directed at Tami. The kiss he had given her in her office played out in her head and time stood still as her lips tingled in anticipation.

In her state of drink-induced euphoria, Trey was no longer irritating and was even charming. Tami continued her commentary, but Trey never took his eyes off of Sandra.

The storm brewing between them was slow and delicious as the heat that had flooded her stomach continued to spread throughout her body. Her breathing became shallow and her heart picked up pace, pounding away to the age-old chemistry between man and woman. The ends of her fingers tingled and her lips had parted slightly of their own accord. She licked them purposefully while focusing on Trey's lips fully aware she was flirting with danger. The need to touch him and kiss him had her fingertips burning for the contact.

For several seconds they stared at each other, enjoying the naked truth mirrored in each other's eyes. If Tami hadn't demanded Trey's attention again, Sandra wasn't so sure they wouldn't have jumped each other on the spot completely disregarding the fact they were in a public place.

The broken spell startled Sandra and she quickly took a sip, berating herself for her weakness.

"Excuse me."

She stood up to head for the restroom. Trey stood as well and she wasn't sure if her knees would hold her. She had forgotten for the moment that Trey or Danny would have to go with her. Between the alcohol and her awareness of Trey, she was having a tough time processing her thoughts and putting them in order. She wasn't sure she could speak to Trey, but there wasn't a whole lot she could do without raising questions.

"I...uh...I have to go to the restroom."

"Me, too."

No one at the table seemed to think it was odd that both of them were heading to the bathrooms. She had mainly wanted to create some breathing space between her and Trey. If she suddenly changed her mind, there might be questions.

Sandra managed to pass by Trey on somewhat steady legs. She hoped she could actually walk to the restroom without bouncing off the walls since he was closely following her down the narrow hallway. Sandra was pleased when she only had to use the wall once to steady herself.

She pushed through the door of the women's restroom and knew Trey would simply take up a post outside the door. She squinted at her reflection in the mirror.

"Girl, you have some serious problems."

She rubbed at her smudged makeup and fluffed her hair. She washed her hands after making use of the facility and used the damp towel to pat the back of her neck in an effort to cool off. Closing her eyes, she took two deep breaths, letting them out slowly in an attempt to straighten out her drunken brain cells. She rarely drank alcohol and now realized why. Give her one drink and she couldn't stop smiling. Give her one more and she felt loopy and apparently flirty. Add a handsome man to that mix and he derailed her thought process.

She breathed in and out a few more times and decided she had better leave before Trey came barging in. Hitching her purse to her shoulder, she squared herself, ready for the rest of the evening. She had had her last drink. Alcohol was not her friend tonight.

Opening the door, she found Trey where she had expected, leaning against the wall with arms crossed. Her body immediately betrayed her when she made eye contact with him. He oozed masculinity and those warm feelings she had tempered moments ago came rushing back, running through every nerve ending. She wondered how much more electricity her nerves could possibly endure until everything was shot to hell or simply exploded. Thank God words weren't necessary because her mouth had gone dry and she used the last of her saliva to lick her dry lips.

The movement wasn't lost on him as his eyes dropped to her mouth. Her adrenaline jumped into overdrive and she felt light-headed. She used the wall to steady herself. The kiss he had given her in the office was still fresh and she wondered if he was remembering the moment as well.

She pushed away from the wall and refocused on returning to the table. She had never felt such chemistry with a man before and had to remind herself it was simply a physical attraction, with a lot of alcohol.

He hadn't given her much room to pass and as she went to do so, her arm brushed up against him. The current almost took her to her knees. She stumbled and Trey quickly caught her by the arm. His hand was wrapped around her upper arm and when she slowly raised her eyes and met his, she knew she was a goner. He was staring at her with more than professional interest and she knew the desire she was feeling showed in her eyes.

For the second time in the thirty-six hours since she had met him, this man who had inserted himself into her life for her protection, put his hand on her neck and drew her to him. This time he didn't hesitate before kissing her. He didn't give her time to back out. This time he took what he wanted.

Sandra matched his hunger and took pleasure in the protective way he wrapped his arms around her. Her hands were pressed against his chest and she marveled even in her state of stupor the physical strength she felt. He was warm and solid and giving. Oh how she had missed this kind of contact.

He tasted of beer nuts. Salty and yummy. His kisses were warm and inviting and it didn't take much persuasion on his part for her to open her lips to receive him fully.

Sandra wasn't sure if she would be able to stop if he decided to elevate their interaction.

Before the thought had fully developed, she felt the warmth of his hands on the bare skin of her back. She could have wept with joy at the feel of the skin-to-skin contact.

"Well, well. This puts a whole new meaning to the term "kissing cousins". Let me know if you need any help on the welcoming committee."

Frank had made it down the hallway without either of them hearing him. Trey pulled away from Sandra, capturing her eyes with his, but didn't release her.

"No need, Frank, she has it covered."

"You go, girl!" And with a snap of his fingers he stepped into the men's restroom.

"Okay, we have a problem."

"I thought that went very well."

Sandra smiled at him, knowing full well the alcohol was talking, but she couldn't seem to shut it up. She wanted to capture this moment forever in a bottle so she could relive the experience. To have the moment spoiled by words of caution was not what she wanted. Life should always be this good, where there was no bad and no worries. There really should be world peace.

"You do know you're going to regret this in the morning." Trey still hadn't released her.

"The kiss? I doubt it."

"The kiss and how much you've been drinking. You'll hate me again."

"I don't hate you, Walker." Even she could tell she was slurring her words. Two drinks and nothing to eat had probably not been a good idea. "You're not very nice most of the time, is all."

"Come daylight you'll be regretting this, Johnson."

"Will you regret it, Walker?"

Chapter 10

Sandra woke to the weight of Tiny's head resting on her chest, his big paws on the bed. She held her head with both hands willing her eyes to open. The night before came rushing back and she groaned. Tiny lifted his head. She scratched him behind one ear.

"It's okay, boy, mama overdid the drinking last night."

She managed to pry her eyes open even though her eyelids hurt from the effort. She squinted to see Tiny better and watched as first one eyebrow then another lifted quizzically, his dark brown eyes never once leaving her face, his ears at attention. His head was tilted as if in question.

"Hey, boy, did you think I wasn't getting up?"

He barked in response causing Sandra to moan and grab her head again. The headache she was refusing to acknowledge pounded in response to the volume of the bark. Trey's words of wisdom came rushing back. He was right and she hated it.

She had always been a lightweight when it came to drinking, so that second drink had not been wise. Placing the blame on Trey seemed like the best bet. He had been driving her crazy with his rules and regulations. And those lips. Especially those lips.

Around each corner he tried to bully her into doing this or that. It seemed like a good reason to throw caution to the wind and thumb her nose at him. Why she had thought throwing caution to the wind meant drinking too much didn't make a lot of sense in the light of day.

Then she remembered their kiss and again she moaned, rolled over in the bed and covered her head with a pillow.

The night wouldn't have been quite so bad if she hadn't acted like a slut. If she remembered correctly, she had practically devoured him. God, he had tasted good, though.

That thought made her sit up too quickly causing Tiny to bark again. She grabbed her head again, afraid it was going to fall off from the pounding.

"Boy, stop, please stop."

"Johnson, you okay?" The rap on the door made Tiny give another sharp bark.

"Tiny!"

Sandra prayed Trey wouldn't open the door. If her head felt this bad, she was pretty sure she was not physically at her best. Sweeping her hand over her hair, she could feel the tangled state her curls were in and figured the makeup she hadn't taken off was everywhere but where it should be.

"Yeah, I'm fine." She whispered to Tiny. "See what you did?" He cocked his head to one side, lifting an eyebrow. "Don't try to act innocent."

"Coffee's on if you need some."

Coffee sounded divine, but Sandra wasn't going to give him the satisfaction of knowing how badly she wanted some.

"Thanks. I'll be out in a bit to grab a cup."

"Would you like an aspirin chaser with that?"

She heard his chuckle. "Go away, Walker."

The only morning rituals she managed to accomplish before going to work were a shower and saying hello to Mr. Ferguson. Ever since Mr. Ferguson had lost his wife the year before, Sandra hadn't missed a morning to say hello.

Her early morning run had been out of the question, not only because she had slept in, but because the thought of adding pounding feet to her pounding head wasn't exactly inviting.

The sunglasses she put on the moment they left the house helped somewhat. But she had to relinquish them when her first client showed up. The clanging of the weight machine was a constant reminder of her overindulgence and made Sandra wonder if weights could be made out of Styrofoam.

After grimacing several times from the clang of the weights, she caught Trey smiling her direction, taking obvious pleasure from her discomfort. She did her best to ignore him, deciding the repercussions of drinking were better than focusing on their kiss. Trey hadn't mentioned anything this morning about either the kiss or the drinking. The aspirin reference and his smug smiles during morning hours had been enough of a reminder.

Sandra started feeling a little better after drinking loads of water and even managed to focus on her books by early afternoon. The phone rang during Lacy's lunchtime, so Sandra picked it up, ready to talk to a client.

"Hey, honey, how are you doing?"

"Mom? Why are you calling me at work? Are you and Dad okay?"

"I saw on the news that Mark had escaped from prison. They think he is heading your way. Sandra, I think you should come stay here for a few days until he's caught."

The last thing Sandra needed was to be coddled by her mother. Donna Johnson had practically sent her over the edge while she was recovering from the first episode with Mark. Her mother thought that by doing everything for Sandra she would recover faster. She hadn't quite grasped that Sandra needed to do the work in order to get better. Going home to mom was not an option if she wanted to keep her sanity. For the first time, Sandra was thankful that Trey and Danny were with her.

"Mom, that won't be necessary. I have two U.S. Marshals watching out for me. But thanks for the offer."

"Well, they can't possibly watch you twenty-four hours a day."

"Yeah, Mom, that's pretty much what they do. They have to live, eat and breathe with me twenty-four/seven until Mark is caught."

There was a long pause. Sandra waited patiently for Donna to finishing putting the puzzle pieces together.

"You...you mean they have to stay with you? In your house?"

"Yes, Mom." Sandra rested her forehead in the palm of her hand and closed her eyes wondering when the last of the headache would be gone.

"Oh, my gosh, what must your neighbors think? Oh, honey, a single woman entertaining two men for several days?"

"Mom, I'm not entertaining them and I don't care what the neighbors think. If they have a problem, they will eventually get over it."

"I don't know—you know how the gossip mill runs."

Sandra knew exactly how the gossip mill ran. The mill usually started and ended with Donna Johnson. She didn't think any less of her mother because of that since she had learned to live with her mother's ways growing up. Her mom had known more about what happened at high school than Sandra had when she attended. There had been times when Sandra wondered if her mother had started rumors just to have something to discuss with her friends.

On the other hand, her mother's interference had taught her

the value of ignoring off-handed remarks and to move forward more quickly rather than dwell on the past. That at least was one thing she had in her favor as she recovered from her injuries and Mark's betrayal. Without knowing it, her mother had given her the fortitude to persevere through anything.

"You know things like that don't bother me, so I should be fine. But I'll call you if anything changes." Sandra knew the right words to pacify her meddling mother, or at the very least side-track her. Another survival skill she could thank her for.

"Well, if you're sure, honey."

"I'm sure. Oh, I have to go, Mom, a client came in. I'll talk to you later. Thanks for the call. Bye."

Sandra hung up and stared at the phone. She knew from experience her mother had barely hung up before dialing one of her many friends to share the latest news, no doubt exaggerating how Sandra was feeling. She knew there would be comments about how "poor Sandra" was having problems sleeping and eating and was extremely distraught over the whole thing. Now she had the added benefit of telling how she was being protected by not one, but two Marshals. After all, her daughter had been a key Federal witness. Sandra chuckled. Her mother was easy to predict.

"Want to share the joke?"

Startled, she found Trey in his usual stance leaning against the doorjamb, arms crossed. In forty-eight hours, he had gone from being a pain in the butt to a pool of warmth in her stomach every time she caught a glimpse of him. Her physical reaction bothered her. He wasn't the only good-looking man she had ever met. There were thousands of them out in the world. She supposed she could blame her reaction on the leftover alcohol in her system or the kiss from last night because nothing else seemed to make sense.

He wasn't even remotely her type. Her previous relationships had been with corporate men who were personable and had a sense of humor.

But Trey didn't fit those parameters. He was the complete opposite. His physical presence alone took up so much space he seemed to suck the air out of a room. That had to be the only explanation for why she felt breathless when she was near him. Her previous relationships seemed soft now compared to Trey. Frank had hit the nail on the head last night when he had mentioned at one point that Trey was "yummy". If the kiss was any indication, then Sandra was in consensus with him. He was definitely yummy. She licked her lips at the memory and was flooded once more with warmth.

"No. I was laughing at something my mom said." In an effort to take her mind off the effect Trey had on her, she asked, "Where's Danny?"

He pushed off from the door and in two steps was at her desk and making himself comfortable in the chair across from her. Although the desk was between them, she leaned back in an effort to distance herself even further. His presence was impossible not to feel.

He appeared relaxed while she felt as tight as a guitar string on the verge of snapping. If that happened, somebody could get hurt.

"He took Lacy to lunch."

"Really. The big, bad boss let someone go have some fun?" Sandra raised an eyebrow and smiled. "Does that mean you're getting soft?"

"No, that means I needed some distance from him. I swear, he may not live through this assignment."

"Patience, Walker, patience. It's a virtue in case you need a reminder."

"What little I had was gone within the first two hours of being with him."

Sandra laughed and Trey smiled. And then time stood still. Her laughter died and her mouth dried out as they stared at each other. Sandra wondered, somewhere in the recesses of her mind, if a client who walked in right now would be able to see the heat between them. This time, she knew she wasn't mistaken. He was attracted to her. The reflection in his eyes had darkened. It was the same passion she had seen last night, right before he had kissed her.

Her mind registered the sound of the wall clock ticking the seconds off. Time was lost on her, though, as the spell she was under seemed impenetrable. She licked her lips and felt the desire hit her deep in the gut as his eyes slid to her mouth. His eyes spoke volumes as they clouded deeper in passion.

"Hey, we're back. Where are you guys?"

Sandra blinked, as the spell was broken. Trey was frowning.

Inwardly she sighed, knowing he was back into full Marshal mode. Although she liked the side of him that was human rather than the robotic persona of his job, she knew he would do all he could to continue to keep it professional. That was for the best. His job here would be over soon and that would be the end of whatever was brewing between them. Better to move on with her life and forget the chemistry between them. There was nothing there to base any kind of continuing relationship on. Outside of the chemistry that smoldered between them, they couldn't even stand each other. Simply relying on sexual attraction would be like chasing rainbows and unicorns.

Trey left her office without saying a word. Sandra leaned forward and placed her head in her hands and closed her eyes. What was wrong with her? She didn't need to complicate her life. She had been placing the blame on Trey Walker, when in reality she needed to move past this temporary glitch. She hadn't been good in chemistry at school and was worse at applying it in real life. Mark Franklin was a perfect example. She couldn't trust her feelings. Trey was right to ignore what was happening and stick to his job. She needed to do the same.

"Hey, boss lady, do you want some lunch?"

Danny was leaning in through the door holding a Subway sandwich bag.

"Sure. Thank you."

Danny placed the bag on her desk and turned to leave but stopped at the doorway. "Are you okay, Sandra?"

"Yeah, why do you ask?"

"You seem.... Um... kinda sad is all."

THE RATTY HOTEL Mark Franklin found himself in was not helping his mood. He didn't have a lot of choices, though. Staying at four-star hotels was out of the question since he needed to keep a low profile.

Although the room smelled clean, he was still apprehensive as to how sterile any of the surfaces were in the room. The curtains were so shabby and faded that it was hard to distinguish what the original color had been. The tile in the bathroom was stained extensively and the carpet had been so heavily used that sections had been worn to threads.

Wishing he had tongs to pull the bedspread back, he instead used his thumb and forefinger to pull it gingerly to one side. Not surprisingly, the sheets were also worn, but did appear to at least be clean. He finished pulling the spread off the bed, leaving it pooled on the floor at the end of the bed. The bedspread had to be the filthiest item in the room and Mark refused to have the blanket anywhere near his skin.

Satisfied that he could stand the room for one night, he proceeded to order a pizza. He was sick of pizza and Chinese food, but couldn't take the chance of showing his face in public any more then was necessary. Right now a prime rib dinner with mashed potatoes and fresh vegetables would be the ultimate treat. However, any thoughts of a luxury meal would have to wait until after Sandra Johnson had been taken care of and he was safe in Mexico.

He flipped through the television channels and paused on the national news broadcast. There, larger than life, was video footage of him from the trial walking into the courtroom cuffed from behind with additional tape showing his reaction when the verdict was read. Turning the volume up, he listened as they repeated what he had heard earlier at the parts store. He was relieved to discover they didn't have anything new on him and were continuing to follow leads. He started pacing in the confined space going over what the next few days held.

Things were going to become more difficult from here on out. The closer he came to his destination, the denser the police force. It was going to be trickier to avoid the cops. For a second, he questioned whether he should just skip the country rather than spend his energy tracking Sandra down. But the thought left as quickly as it had come. The anger he felt over the hell she had put him through had only intensified over time. His need for revenge would only be satisfied once this mission was complete.

A fire burned in the pit of his stomach at the resentment he felt towards Sandra and how she had forever changed his life. She was the one who had deliberately taken his luxurious lifestyle away from him and that bitch would pay for it.

The knock at the door interrupted his thoughts. Checking the keyhole, he verified that the person on the other side really was the pizza guy. Mark lowered the bill of his hat and opened the door, money already in hand. The less contact the better.

Stars were starting to pepper the black canvas of the sky and a crescent moon hung off to one side. Mark had purposely left only the bathroom light on so that the bedroom area was still dark. There was no other light nearby that he had to worry about that would show his face.

"All meat pizza, sir?"

"Yeah, thanks." Mark shoved the money at the kid.

"Hey, don't I know you?"

Mark froze. "Nope."

"Weird, cause you seem so familiar."

Mark closed the door before the kid could say another word. The conversation only confirmed what Mark already knew. Patience and extra precautions were top priorities. In order to win the prize, he had to be at the top of his game. The attributes that had made him successful in the world of finance would be needed to succeed in this quest as well. His only weakness had been the woman who put him behind bars and he'd be damned if she got away with that.

Chapter 11

Trey spent the rest of the day avoiding Sandra. He had let his attraction for her interfere with his job and he couldn't afford to have that happen again. Why he had given into their physical attraction puzzled him. Twice he had given in. There had been a number of attractive women he had met over the years while on assignment. There had been a few he had been physically attracted to. Each time, he had simply reminded himself he was there to do a job and that was that. Each time the reminder had put a quick end to anything happening. Pleasure was for personal use and never to be mixed with business.

Hell, there had been a number of attractive women walk by the window where he had taken up residence at Sandra's gym. He had sat there for hours with his laptop in order to keep an eye on the streets. Even Frank had wandered down from the bank on his break. In his case, he didn't even try to be subtle. He came directly into Sandra's business. With a "Hey, big guy" and a wink and smile, he'd chatted with Sandra and Logan for a few minutes. When he left, he stopped at the door long enough to mutter something about "scrumptious in a tight pair of jeans" and left with another wink and a wiggle of his fingers.

Trey wasn't naïve. He knew women, and apparently some men, were attracted to him so there was no reason to wonder why one or two women kept walking by, each time more brazen then the last. One of them had written her number on the palm of her hand and stopped long enough to show him, then motioned with her thumb and pinky to call her. None of them affected him.

Not for the first time that day, he ran a hand through his hair out of frustration over his reaction to Sandra. His response was unprofessional and unacceptable. She was just another woman. Her voice carried to him as she gave instructions and encouragement to a client. He watched her as she pushed her client to finish the reps. A surge of desire rushed through him as he watched her slap raised hands with the client in a moment of triumph. Her smile was genuine and contagious and even that irritated him because that only reminded him of her lips responding to his kiss. *Damn it.*

His scowl remained in place, leaving no room in anyone's mind that they were better off not to approach him. With the exception of taking his frustration out on Logan, he kept talking to a minimum. Logan visibly jumped when Trey so much as cleared his throat.

"Logan, you belong at the front of the building watching the streets, not helping Lacy."

"I was showing her a short cut on the computer."

"We're not here to socialize, we are here to do a job. Get back where you belong."

For once Logan didn't talk back, only glancing at Lacy to give an apologetic shrug before taking up his position at the store-front windows.

Trey didn't have to look at Sandra to know what her reaction was to him barking orders. If she had it her way, he would be coddling Logan instead of teaching him how the job was done in a professional manner. There wasn't any room to get distracted, no matter how soft the assignment may seem. Every job had danger lurking around the corner and dropping your guard was dangerous.

In the forty-eight hours since they had been thrown together, he had come to know all too well that she disapproved of the way he handled Logan. Trey kept his head focused on the job at hand tempering any emotions he might have for her. After all this was a job, not a dating service. As the day progressed, he was finally able to focus directly on the job and keep Sandra in the client column where she belonged.

The agency still didn't have any idea of Franklin's whereabouts, which added to Trey's aggravation. He knew they were scrambling and had the best people working on the case, but he had never known it to take this long to at least find a trail. Franklin seemed to have disappeared off the face of the earth.

On the other hand, Franklin had shown himself to be incredibly bright. He was proving to be the weasel that had earned himself a place behind bars to begin with. Underhanded and sly, he continued to fly under their radar and Trey was itching to personally get his hands on him. He wanted this assignment over for a variety of reasons and Franklin was becoming a barb he needed ripped from his side.

For the rest of the afternoon, Trey worked on his computer, keeping up with his other projects and typing his daily notes. When he finally took time to stretch and relieve the tension in his shoulders and his back, he saw Logan emerging from the massage room with drops of oil on his jeans.

———

"Danny, why do you feel the need to continue to get into my massage oils?"

"I wanted to give Lacy a foot massage. She's been on her feet all day and I thought it would be a nice thing to do for her." He glanced over at Lacy, puppy love written on his face.

Perhaps Trey had been right, Sandra thought with a shudder. Maybe she should have left the match making alone. She would never admit that to Trey, though. There was no reason to give him any further gloating material. She had really just wanted to boost Danny's confidence since she had known that Lacy would be nice to him. Trey certainly wasn't helping Danny in that department. But Sandra hadn't expected Lacy to become enamored with him. She watched Lacy wiggle her fingers at Danny, who was smiling ear-to-ear.

Sandra let out a sigh and rubbed her temples. She was exhausted. She'd used every ounce of strength and determination to fight off the hangover as well as the confusing and mixed messages she seemed to pick up from Trey. Finally after a lot of self-talk throughout the day she had managed to put him back into the compartment of her brain saved for people she didn't want to waste time thinking about.

She stepped into the massage room to survey Danny's latest disaster. Thankfully the mess wasn't as big as his last spill, but once again, he had some on his jeans as well as his hands.

"Go wash the oil off your hands and I'll take care of this."

"You don't have to do that, Sandra. It was my fault, I can clean it up."

"I'll have most of this taken care of before you get it off you."

Sandra watched as he carefully avoided the oil on the floor and walked over to the sink to soap up. Grabbing one of the rags off a shelf, she proceeded to clean up the excess oil before taking soap and water to the floor to wipe up the residue.

Massages were scheduled for the days Lacy came in for work

so there was always someone at the front desk while she was behind closed doors. Those particular days were especially busy, leaving little time for Sandra to do anything but personal training and massages. Having to add clean up duty on her busiest day took precious time from returning phone calls.

She liked these busy days, though, because of the energy that came from the chatter of clients dishing on the latest news and gossip around town. She felt connected to the city when she had opportunities to connect with her clients. She considered many of them to be friends. Without them realizing it, they had helped her through some dark moments as she recovered emotionally from her past.

Today hadn't been normal, though. The two men who had entered her life reminded her once again of her past. One of them seemed to create more work for her while the other made her feel emotions she thought were dormant forever. She and Trey had managed to avoid each other for the remainder of the afternoon, but Sandra could feel him. While working with a client she knew where he was even when he wasn't in her view. Too many times she had glanced in his direction to find his eyes on her with the scowl permanently etched on his forehead.

The weight room wasn't especially big. It was big enough, though, for Sandra to have the latest equipment and still move with ease around it. The desk Lacy occupied three days a week was near the door so she could greet the clients and, if necessary, set up for their massage or circuit training if Sandra was running behind schedule. Everything ran like clockwork. She liked her schedule that way. Being organized gave her a sense of balance and order. Today, however, she wasn't feeling balanced or orderly. Leaning back on her heels, she viewed her progress. Danny was finishing his own clean up and in doing so had gotten his jeans soaking wet. At least this time it wasn't his dress pants. The oil wouldn't leave a stain on the denim like it had on his other pants.

Sandra glanced behind her to see Lacy standing in the doorway, holding paperwork in one hand and a stapler in the other. Her eyes darted between Sandra and Danny, her mouth dropping open a little when she saw his pants.

"I dropped the massage oil." Again, the puppy dog eyes.

"Oh, man." Lacy pressed the papers to her chest. Sandra didn't know whether to laugh or cry. She took care of a few more spots before deciding the room was back to normal.

"I'm so sorry. You should have yelled. I would have cleaned up the floor."

As Lacy stepped into the room to help, Trey appeared, taking up the entire space of the doorway. He was holding the doorjamb above him, leaning into the room. Sandra was going to have to have a serious talk with her heart about consistently betraying her every time Trey came close.

"It's six. Are you done for the day?"

She sighed letting out the breath she had been holding. "Yes, I'm done for the day." She laid the towels flat on top of the washer and dryer, knowing she couldn't wash them until she returned in the morning.

She sent up another silent prayer that Trey's phone would ring soon with the news that Mark had been caught. The man was wreaking havoc on her life and her nerves and she wanted her normal routine back.

Danny and Lacy had left the room as Sandra finished putting items back in place. Lacy returned shortly to let her know her mom was on the phone again. Sandra returned to her office for the inevitable guilt-laced lecture.

"Mom, is there something wrong?" Sandra knew there wasn't, but she hoped the question would throw her off enough she would forget the real reason why she called.

"Well, I do have a sore throat. I understand there is some awful cold going around."

Sandra smiled to herself. It didn't take much to distract her mom. "Oh, I'm sorry to hear that. How long have you had it?"

"I woke up with it this morning. It was really painful first thing, but it's not so annoying now."

Her mind drifted when she saw Trey walk past her door, while her mom listed off the rest of her symptoms. She made the appropriate sounds of concern for her mom's benefit, not retaining a thing she rattled on about.

Something her Mom said brought her back around. "What did you say?"

"Honey, please pay attention."

"Sorry, I was distracted for a moment."

"I was saying that my friend, Maggie, you remember, Maggie don't you? She was the widow down the street that slept around a lot. I was the only one of her friends that stuck by her during her indiscretions."

Yes, Sandra remembered. Her Mom would be on the phone one minute talking to a friend about how inappropriately Maggie was behaving, and the next telling Maggie not to pay any attention to the gossip. Sandra could feel her headache coming back.

"Mom, back to your point."

"Well, Maggie thinks your father should come stay with you."

Sandra found herself rubbing her temple with her free hand, wanting desperately to bang her head on the desk. "What does Dad think?"

"He thinks I'm being overprotective and insists that you're a big girl and can take care of yourself." Sandra heard her draw a deep breath, knowing she wasn't finished. "He figures the two strangers with you are plenty of protection and has absolutely no concern about them causing gossip while they stay with you."

Before she could continue her rant, Sandra interrupted her. "Mom, he's right. I am a big girl. And they are not just any strangers, they are U.S. Marshals who are trained to protect people. That's what they are here for, so you need to take a deep breath and relax. Chances are that by this time tomorrow, Mark will be back in jail and they will be gone."

"Well, I hope so."

"It'll be fine, Mom. Go make Dad some dinner and enjoy the rest of your evening."

"If you're sure."

"I'm sure. Bye, Mom. Love you."

Sandra stared at the phone, wondering how the child/parent relationship could be reversed so easily. She stood and straightened her desk for the next day's work. She left her office after shutting down the computer, switching the light off and closing the door. Trey and Danny were waiting for her at the front door. From the frying pan into the fire, she thought as she walked toward them.

Suddenly, a loud noise from outside startled Sandra and propelled Trey into action. Suddenly, she found herself wrapped in Trey's arms as he took them both to the hard floor. He took the brunt of her weight before rolling on top of her protectively. He had even thought to place his hand at the back of her head so when they rolled she wouldn't bump her head.

The loud noise replayed over and over in her head as she lay on the floor waiting for air to fill her lungs and for her heart to stop racing. *Was that a gunshot?*

Even though Trey had taken the brunt of the fall, she knew her elbow and perhaps her shoulder would make her pay for it later. She glanced over and saw Danny crouched with his gun drawn. The tote bag she had been carrying sat upright beside him, looking like she had casually placed it in that spot, rather than having dropped the bag as Trey tackled her.

"Are you okay?"

She nodded her head, and he rolled off her, gun drawn. Immediately she missed the warmth and security of his body. He told her to stay put, which was fine since she was still shaking.

The noise came again, this time further down the street. It was just a vehicle backfiring. Trey and Danny rose cautiously and went through the front door to verify the source of the noise. A few seconds later, they returned and Sandra had yet to move. She might be in shock or perhaps it was pure exhaustion, but either way, she knew there was no strength left for her to stumble to her feet on her own.

They both helped her up and she instantly felt dizzy. She paused to rest her hands on her knees and drop her head, taking some deep breaths till the dizziness passed.

Perhaps the realization that Mark could really take her out at any moment had finally penetrated her thick head. She had an overwhelming urge to burst into tears when she looked at Trey and Danny. She managed to choke back the emotion and gave them a weak smile.

Trey took her arm. "Are you sure you're okay?"

She could only nod, afraid if she spoke she would start crying.

"Let's go home."

Sandra had never been so thankful to have someone take over her life. She felt numb. Shivering, she followed Trey out the door with Danny behind her. When she tried to lock the door, she found she was shaking too much to put the key into the lock. Trey wrapped his hand around hers to steady her shaking and help her guide the key into the hole.

His kindness was almost her undoing, but again she found

some internal strength to stuff the tears down before they spilled over. After replacing the key in her purse, Trey grabbed her hand and led her to the car, helping her into the back and fastening her seatbelt. Not once did he say anything, as if he knew she would lose her control. Even Danny managed to keep from talking. Sandra was thankful for the silence.

The sound had simply been the backfire of a car. Why was this upsetting her so much? She trusted Trey and Danny to protect her. They had proven how reliable they were. She closed her eyes to let the seriousness of the situation fully settle into her mind. Demons she believed she had tossed away for good had resurfaced. She did her slow breathing, concentrating on each breath and gathering inner strength.

The stark truth was Mark Franklin was an evil man who was once again trying to destroy her life. Rebuilding her confidence and her life had taken months after his attempt on her life. And then, Trey and Danny had shown up and denial was the cement wall she had hidden behind.

Sandra's levelheaded side fought down the part of her that wanted to collapse into a fetal position on her bed and remain there until Mark was captured. He had taken so much from her before because she hadn't seen it coming. There was no reason to permit him to blindside her again. This time she knew what was happening and she needed to use that knowledge to her advantage.

———

TREY KEPT an eye on Sandra in the rearview mirror as he drove carefully back to her place, still mindful of what was going on around him. He could see the play of emotions on her face. The pit of his stomach ached and he rubbed his sternum hoping to relieve the indigestion that seemed to have settled there. Thankfully Danny had enough sense to keep quiet and was also surveying the streets.

Trey pulled up to the curb in front of Sandra's house and unbuckled his seatbelt before the car came to a standstill. Danny followed his example.

"Go around the back of the house and check out the perimeter while we go in through the front."

Danny nodded and slid out of the car. Trey exited and opened the door for Sandra. Her eyes were still closed and didn't open until he leaned across her to unbuckle her seatbelt. She was still pale. He was close enough to see the rim of light green surrounding her brown eyes. Blinking several times, she finally seemed to realize she was home.

He took her hand, helping her to the sidewalk, steadying her once. She stood and straightened her shoulders as Trey released her. She managed a weak smile in his direction before heading to the front door. He followed, continuing to scan their surroundings.

Stepping in front of her, he unlocked the door and went inside, pulling Sandra directly behind him. Tiny greeted them with a yawn and stretch and a swish of his tail as he stood up and padded over to them. While Sandra greeted the dog, Trey closed and locked the door before heading to the slider in the kitchen. Sandra followed him so when Trey opened the slider to let Danny in, Tiny slipped outside to do his own perimeter check.

Sandra went through the motions of filling a cup with water and nuking it in the microwave. Trey left the kitchen as Sandra stood watching her cup rotate in the microwave.

"Everything okay?" Trey asked the question softly to Danny.

"Yeah. The backyard was quiet."

"I'm going to check in with the office."

A few minutes later Trey disconnected from his phone.

"Nothing. Absolutely nothing." He closed his eyes briefly. "This is insane. We are usually all over a situation like this. Franklin should not be outsmarting an agency with the best people working for them."

"It's only been forty-eight hours, Boss."

"Forty-eight hours too long." Trey needed an outlet. "I'm going to go for a run while there's still light. Can you hold things down here for a half hour?"

"Not a problem."

By the time he returned, Tiny had taken up his spot by the closed door of Sandra's bedroom, his ears perked. Trey gave him a pat on the head as he walked by to take a shower. "Good boy."

———

IMMERSED in a hot tub of sudsy water with a cup of tea, Sandra willed her body to relax. Once behind the closed door of her bedroom, she had finally given into tears. As she suspected, her left elbow and shoulder were sore.

Replaying the moment in her mind, she was in awe at how quickly Trey and Danny had both reacted. That should have been comforting, but the image kept reminding her of how vulnerable she was. Her feelings vacillated between terror and anger. She was angry at how Mark Franklin had once again become the center of her life, and terrified, remembering how close he had come to killing her.

When the water had cooled, Sandra roused herself to climb out of the tub with nothing resolved. She felt more aches then she had noticed at first, her muscles protesting when she stood. Drying herself off, she wrapped herself in her oversized bathrobe, deciding she was too tired to eat or socialize. The guys were on their own, even though she knew she didn't really have to cater to them.

Sandra found some comfort in the familiarity of her bed when she climbed in and buried herself in the covers. She fell asleep quickly she was so physically and emotionally exhausted.

She didn't hear Trey open her door to let Tiny in to take his place next to her bed. When he gently swept a stray hair off her face, she didn't feel his touch. When he whispered "sweet dreams," she didn't feel his breath on her cheek.

"Take care of her, boy."

Tiny lifted his head as if he understood.

———

LOUD NOISES PENETRATED Sandra's sleep. Reaching over, she tried to turn off her alarm but to no avail. Tiny nudged her hand, trying to attract her attention. "What is it, Tiny?"

Sandra realized she had been woken by raised voices. *Oh man, please let this be a dream.*

Sandra reached for the running gear she kept near her bed. She barely finished pulling it on when her bedroom door was thrown open, letting light from the family room spill onto her carpet. Sandra blinked to focus. The short, trim woman standing at the door hustled over, embracing her in a bear hug.

"Sweetie, thank goodness you're safe."

Sandra returned the hug, patting her mom on the back. "Of course I'm safe. I told you I was."

The overhead light to her room came on. Marshal Walker did not appear to be happy. Glancing at her clock, she noted that it was one in the morning. She managed to unwind herself from her mom's over-zealous embrace.

"Mom, it's one in the morning. Why are you here? Is Dad okay?"

"This couldn't wait. I had a premonition."

"Premonition?" Sandra raised an eyebrow at her mother, avoiding eye contact with Trey.

Her mother was petite and appeared perfectly harmless, but could be a bulldog when she set her mind on something. Sandra pressed her lips together and put her fingers over them to keep from smiling. Donna Johnson had managed to bully herself past Trey Walker. The yin and yang of the universe facing off.

Although 61, her mother appeared at least ten years younger thanks to good genes, good hair color and good skin products. She kept fit and was stronger than she appeared.

Thinking how the standoff must have gone when Trey opened the door to find her mother standing outside took the edge off the day she had. She shook her head. Trey hadn't stood a chance with her mother from the minute he opened the door. The fact that she was standing in front of Sandra was proof positive. As irritating as her mother could be, Sandra loved her tenacity.

"Yes, premonition. You know how I get those once in a while and they always come true."

The only time Sandra remembered her mother predicting anything had been the death of her great grandmother. Who wouldn't have guessed that? The woman had been ninety-eight and in the hospital with pneumonia.

"Okay, I'll bite. What was your premonition, Mom?"

"I had a strong sense that Mark was coming here to hurt you, so Maggie and I came to take you home."

Mentally, Sandra rolled her eyes. Most adult children would be concerned that their parent was showing signs of dementia, but her mom wasn't a typical parent. "Maggie came with you?"

"Hi, Sandra."

Maggie stood at the bedroom door behind Trey. While Donna Johnson dressed herself in casual classic attire, Maggie McDougal dressed more like a hooker, though not because she was one. Tonight she wore skin-tight jeans, three-inch red heels and a deep black cowl neck sweater advertising her assets.

For as long as Sandra had known her, Maggie had worn her hair long and blond with an abundance of soft curls and as high as Dolly Parton. Tonight was no different with the added benefit of a big red flower holding one side up and out of the way. Somehow she managed to carry off the look. Other woman in their late fifties would never have been able to do that. They would have had been categorized as trailer-park trash. However with Maggie, her fashion sense fit her personality.

Sandra gave her a smile. "Hey, Maggie. It's nice to see you."

She returned her attention to her mother again. "Mom, you heard that information on the television reports and then you and I talked about this. Remember?"

"Oh, I know, honey." She waved her hand at Sandra, dismissing her comment. "It's more than that though. He's not that far away. I can feel it in my bones."

If the situation had been less serious, Sandra would have burst out laughing. But something about her mom's insistence sent cold chills through her body.

"Has your Mom ever been right about her other premonitions?" Trey sounded skeptical. Sandra couldn't blame him, but she refused to embarrass her mother. Instead she took her mother by the shoulders.

"Mom, I understand this scares you, but as you can see, I am well protected with Trey and Danny both here."

Sandra and Trey glanced at Danny and saw him mesmerized by Maggie. Trey's scowl deepened and he cleared his throat, which broke the spell.

"What?"

Trey rolled his eyes and turned back to Sandra. "Can we wrap this up so we can get some sleep?"

"Mom, it's late and Trey's right, we all need to get some sleep."

"Oh, of course. We can settle in the guestroom."

Crap! The thought of adding two more people to this mix was enough to make drinking again sound good. Sandra wasn't sure how to play this.

"Mrs. Johnson, there isn't enough room in Sandra's small house for all of us."

"Of course there isn't. You and, uh, the other fella," Donna waved her hand toward Danny who once again had his eyes fixed on Maggie, "can get a hotel now. Since we're here, you boys don't need to bother with my daughter any longer." She turned and patted Sandra on the cheek as if she was talking about a ten-year old child. "I'll take good care of her."

"Mom it doesn't work that way."

"Mrs. Johnson." Trey took two strides, wrapped his arm around her shoulders, turned her toward the bedroom door and walked her to the family room. "I understand completely your need to protect your daughter. We have a need to protect her as well."

Sandra watched as Trey transformed into a man charming his way into a woman's heart. Just as unbelievable was the fact her mom seemed to be falling for his charm. As she followed them out, she listened while Trey convinced Donna and Maggie that, for their own safety, they should check into a hotel and that the Agency would be more than happy to pick up the bill. That he couldn't take a chance on something happening to them.

Before Sandra knew it, Danny had booked the two older women a room and then left with them to make sure they settled into the hotel. Alone with Trey, she could only gaze at him for a moment.

"Where the hell did you find that guy?"

"What guy?"

"The charming, considerate, soft-spoken guy who convinced one of the most stubborn women I know to do exactly what you wanted. Which, by the way, is exactly the correct angle for dealing with my Mom."

"My job is to be everything to everyone."

"Ah, that explains your pain-in-the-ass attitude with me."

Trey smiled a slow smile. Sandra placed a hand on the flat of her stomach in an effort to squelch the warm embers stirring at the sight. He took a purposeful step towards her and then another as the breath in her lungs was trapped for a moment. She had to peer up at him when he was but mere inches from her. Overwhelmed by his closeness, she felt flustered and could feel heat flushing her face.

He tucked a piece of loose hair neatly behind her ear and then cupped the side of her face. Sandra responded to the warmth and security his hand promised.

"What do you want me to be to you, Sandra?"

Hearing her first name spoken jolted her back to her senses and broke the spell she had fallen under. He really was a chameleon and was dangerously good at the game. She had to steel her heart against the pheromones sparking off him. Well, two could play at that game.

She turned and kissed the palm of his hand and saw victory in his eyes. "I want. Very much. For you. To get the hell out of my life."

With that Sandra spun around, thankful that she was no longer in physical contact with Trey. She called Tiny and marched back into her bedroom. As she closed the door, he smiled at her. Wagging her fingers goodnight, she closed the door and heard him chuckle.

Leaning against the door, she took a moment to catch her breath. That had been too close. She needed to stop lusting after her bodyguard. Other women might throw themselves at Trey

Walker, but she refused to be one of them. Groaning, she pushed herself away from the door and crawled back into bed, burrowing under the covers, wanting something familiar and comforting. Why couldn't the agency send someone less attractive and less male? What happened to equal opportunity? Shouldn't they have sent a woman to do this job?

Tossing and turning, Sandra didn't think sleep would come but finally succumbed sometime after Danny's return. She could hear the low rumble of their voices for a few minutes before the house was quiet again. Although she did sleep, her dreams were restless and filled with Trey and his seductive eyes.

In the morning, prying her eyes open was difficult at best and once more she knew she would not be going for her morning run. If Mark wasn't caught soon, this setup was going to make her lazy and possibly fat.

She pulled herself from the warm bed, realizing she hadn't bothered to change back into her pajamas. The hour on the clock made her wince. She had missed saying hello to Mr. Ferguson. To top it off, Tiny was no longer in the room, which meant Trey had let him out.

Her bare feet sank into the soft carpet as she made her way to the bathroom. She leaned over the sink to look closely at the reflection in the mirror. Her eyes were swollen from lack of sleep. The dark circles, which had appeared the day after Trey had shown up, were worse. It was Friday and she hoped her weekend would start off with the good news that Mark had been caught and she could move on with her life without Trey and Danny underfoot. She didn't stop to analyze why that thought made her feel suddenly lonely.

Chapter 12

Mark Franklin had finally reached his destination. Ferry City was a midsized city with a simple layout. He was running out of patience to finish what he came to do and finally put the last three years behind him.

With his ball cap low and his sunglasses on, he cruised through the town and passed by Sandra's fitness business, *Get to Fit!* It was nine in the morning and there were no signs of life. The downtown business area probably wouldn't wake up until around ten, so Mark turned a few blocks later and wove his way through the alley to case the back of her business.

The alley wasn't paved and had the typical rutted dirt that would make a getaway difficult to leave in a hurry. No one was around, so he parked. He checked the back door. The handle was locked and there was no give when he pushed, which meant the door had one or two deadbolts. The front of the business, he knew, was glass that would make it easy to simply put a bullet through. However, he wanted her to know what was coming. He wanted her to suffer as much as he had over the past several years before he killed her. He wanted her to suffer from physical pain. Slowly. Deliberately.

Mark hit the door in frustration. He now had to hope her home had an easier means of entry. He was going to have to wait until she was at work before he could scope her neighborhood out.

Both her business and home addresses had been easy to obtain through Internet search engines. The last rundown motel he had stayed at surprisingly had a relatively new computer plus high-speed Internet. Very clever, that Internet. The ability to obtain information had grown significantly over the three years of his incarceration. He glanced down the alley both ways before climbing back into the nondescript car he had taken from an old lady.

While dumping the last car, he had only walked a few blocks before noticing the elderly woman puttering in her yard. After striking up a conversation, he had discovered that she was widowed and depended on family and friends to take her places. Although she did have a car, it had been locked in the garage and not used since her husband died several months back.

After a few more minutes of small talk, he had wandered down the street and around the corner until he could dart down the alley and backtrack to her garage. The side door was unlocked.

Once on the open road, he could only smile. That had been the perfect heist. He figured it would be weeks, if not months, before the woman discovered her car was missing. The light brown sedan would take him all the way to Mexico without standing out anywhere.

Mark pulled back onto the main street of Ferry City and cruised further down for a better feel of the town's layout. There were a number of signs posted along the street about an upcoming community dance at the grange hall on Saturday. *Hicks*, he thought. Sad to think that in this day and age a dance at the grange hall was considered entertainment. He would never have been able to handle small town life with only local dances and high school football games to look forward to. The town's only saving grace was a row of six bars within a few miles of each other. That made sense, since the slow pace of life here probably drove people to drink.

Mark parked in front of a doughnut shop a few blocks from Sandra's fitness center. Through the plate glass window, he could see a lot of seniors having their morning gab sessions over coffee. A barstool at the window would be a good place to watch for Sandra's arrival at work.

He exited the car and made his way inside. No one gave him a second glance, exactly as he had hoped. Nodding to the gentlemen at one table, he made his way to the counter, ordered a coffee and then picked a stool at the bar that covered the length of the window.

Twenty minutes later, he was rewarded for the wait. An SUV pulled up to the front of her business. He couldn't see into the vehicle itself, so he was startled when the driver and then the passenger stepped out and neither were Sandra. She alighted from the back seat on the passenger's side.

The driver was tall and fit. Although dressed casually, his gut feeling told Mark the relationship between Sandra and the driver was not a personal one.

The passenger was an awkward-looking gentleman. He appeared to be in his twenties and oblivious to the world around him. He was dressed casually in jeans and a T-shirt with a light jacket.

Mark frowned and took a sip of his coffee. What the hell was going on? Who were these guys? He watched while the driver took the key from Sandra, noting that she was between the two guys. While the driver opened the door to the business, the awkward guy had his back to them, surveying the street.

Shit! He watched the driver walk into the business while

Sandra and the geek waited outside. When the tall one returned, he motioned them to enter. Mark hadn't figured that the government would give her bodyguards. *Damn it!*

He managed to control the urge to slam his fist on the counter. Anger would not help him. Keeping his cool was critical and getting mad over an unexpected turn of events would not be productive.

Taking a deep breath, he let it out slowly and managed to tamp down the anger. The street became busier as owners arrived to open their shop doors. A car pulled up in front of Sandra's and a pretty young lady hopped out of the car. Long, thick brunette hair hung down her back and the three-inch heels she wore only emphasized how incredibly long her legs were. She was dressed for work and not to work out. An employee maybe? He watched as she approached the door and saw the geek open it with a goofy smile as he let her into the building. She returned the smile, touching him slightly on the arm as she passed him.

Good luck with that, buddy, Mark thought. *She'll screw you somehow and then you'll be left out in the cold.*

So Sandra had one guy to protect her and one gratuitous warm body whose Achilles heel was the brunette? He would be easy enough to deal with. The driver, however, was another story. Rather than worry about dealing with him, Mark was simply going to have to separate Sandra from him. Although in good shape, he wasn't willing to get into a physical altercation with a guy who no doubt carried a gun.

First things first. Now that she was at work, he needed to survey her residence. He would have to kill her at her house after they dropped her off in the evening.

Adjusting his hat, he left the coffee shop and climbed into the car. Cruising back down the main street, he once again glanced into her business and saw her talking to the gal who was now behind the desk at the front.

Sandra's home sat on a quiet street. The day was going to be comfortable and the only neighbor he saw was an elderly gentleman sitting on his porch. He couldn't take a chance and slow down for a good look at the front of her home while the man was outside. He continued down the street a few blocks before he turned.

He once again found himself in an alley. This alley was paved which would make for a better escape. Sandra's backyard was hidden behind a six-foot wooden fence, so at the end of the alley he pulled over and parked the car on the side street.

He glanced around, stepped out of the car and headed back down the alley. He hoped he looked as nondescript as the car and appeared to simply be taking a short cut. He slowed down when he reached Sandra's back yard.

The gate was locked so he was going to have to scale the fence. He found a couple of boards which he stacked and then placed a discarded bucket on top of those. The makeshift bench gave him enough height to gain some leverage and pull himself over the fence. Dropping on the other side, he stayed crouched for a moment so he could take in his surroundings. A squirrel in the tree above him started chattering, but other than that, there were no other signs of life.

He darted across the expanse of lawn and up the cement steps to the sliding glass doors. The blinds were drawn, so seeing inside was impossible and the door was locked. Mark could see a metal rod wedged in the bottom of the slider.

Stepping off the deck, he examined the back of the house more closely, noting the bathroom and probably bedroom on the back end, which meant the family room and perhaps another bedroom were in the front of the house. Not a large house.

He used a lawn chair to reach the bathroom window and then smiled as he pushed on the window and found it unlatched. She was so predictable. Even when they were together, she had hated to keep the window closed while she showered and would forget to lock it when she was done.

Perfect, he thought. When she was asleep, he would be able to ease himself in quietly. He liked the element of surprise. Closing the window, he quickly replaced the chair and left, using one of the branches on the tree in her yard to leverage himself over the fence, while the squirrel continued to scold him.

Chapter 13

As the day progressed, Sandra found her energy being sucked out of her. The hope that Trey would announce any moment they had captured Mark had continued to dwindle as the day progressed and his phone remained silent. When he did check in with the office after lunch, they had finally come up with a solid lead the day before from a motel clerk not more than three hundred miles from Ferry City.

Rather than being excited about the lead, Sandra started to feel the walls closing in on her. Mark was too close. How had they managed to let him get so close? When she wasn't busy with a client she found herself cleaning excessively. Items that were already cleaned were cleaned again. Trey's presence reassured her of her physical safety, but also reminded her that her emotional safety was another matter.

By mid-afternoon she thought she would lose her mind and then her mother and Maggie showed up. She had completely forgotten her mom was in town she'd been so consumed with anxiety. For most people, having their mother close under such circumstances would have been a blessing. Sandra thought a straitjacket and the psych ward seemed like better options.

"Sorry we're late, but Maggie insisted we go shopping first. Who was I to argue?"

"I don't think I can do this Walker," she whispered as Donna Johnson approached her, wanting a hug. She forced a smile as her mom embraced her. Trey gave her an empathetic smile and mouthed to her that everything would be fine.

His understanding at the moment melted the rest of the ice around her heart. She was falling in love with this gruff, aggravating agent she'd known for a mere three days. As much as she had tried to fight the attraction, he had managed to slide under her skin. She choked on her emotions knowing he didn't return her feelings. Tears stung her eyes. This bad habit of falling in love with the wrong guy had to stop.

Pulling away from their embrace, her mom mistook her tears. "Oh honey, everything will be fine."

Donna smoothed the hair from her daughter's cheek and tucked a piece behind her ear. The movement reminded Sandra of Trey doing that at the bar and again last night. She turned to go back to her office before she could no longer hold back the tears. Her mother trailed along behind her. Finding some tissue, Sandra wiped the moisture from her eyes and blew her nose before she turned to her mom.

"Honey, are you okay? It isn't like you to be so emotional."

"I'm okay, really. Thanks for asking. I haven't slept well these past few nights. Between that and being extremely busy at work, I'm exhausted." She managed a reassuring smile for her mom.

She knew her mother really cared, but she was the type of person who was always offering advice and trying to solve your problems.

Sometimes you just needed someone to listen so you could find your own answers. Like Trey had done the first night he was at her house when she woken from the bad dream.

From the pain-in-the-ass guy she had met that first morning

who was all business, to a caring human being who was warm and breathing and allowed her to spill her guts simply by embracing her and offering silent comfort. He had given her permission to express her feelings without editing them the way her mom often did.

It had been a long time since she had felt comfortable enough with anyone to be herself. Maybe this wasn't really love, maybe what she was feeling was just gratitude. Trey had managed to find the bridge between the person she had once been, and the woman she was now. Sandra had liked the person she had been before the fiasco with Mark. But she especially liked the person she had become. She was stronger and smarter now. Trey had managed to make her appreciate what she was capable of and for that she would be eternally grateful.

"I'm really okay, Mom."

Sandra sat at her desk to tackle the paper work in front of her and took a deep breath. She wasn't sure if the reassurance she spoke was for her mom's benefit or hers. Her desire to live life to its fullest and not let Mark dictate how she acted and felt had tilted a little. Now was time to take that back. This was simply a bump in the road. A big bump, but nothing she couldn't endure for a little longer.

The internal pep talk helped and she sat up straighter. The circumstances were ridiculous. She wasn't falling in love with Trey Walker. You don't do that in three days. She was just confusing love with the gratitude she felt. That's all. Trey was simply an attractive man who was in her life for a matter of a few hours longer.

"Things are going to turn out fine. So you're more than welcome to stay in town for a while or go on home." Her stomach ached a little at her conviction over Trey, but she ignored the ache, putting it aside and refusing to explore any more emotions for the day. "If you do stay, you might as well stay through the weekend. We have a community dance planned for tomorrow night with a live band at the grange."

She knew how her mother was always begging her dad to take her dancing. On occasion he would give in, but most of the time Donna only managed a fix by tagging along with her friends.

"Oh," she clapped her hands and beamed from ear-to-ear. "Maggie would love to go to a dance. We will stick around until Sunday then. I'll go tell her. Maggie will probably want to hit the mall again for something new."

Sandra smiled. Her mom preferred to have others believe she would never be so superficial as to want to go shopping for *herself*. Maggie became the easy excuse.

At the door Donna turned, a smile no longer lighting her face. Sandra didn't think she had ever seen her mom so serious.

"I love you, honey, and I know I make it hard for you to be you, but you have always been so fiercely independent that I think I just want you to want your mother. I'm immensely proud of you not only for how much you have accomplished, but also for how much you have had to overcome."

Tears surfaced once again, but Sandra managed to choke out a response after forcing down the lump in her throat. "Thank you, Mom. I think that is the sweetest thing anyone has ever said to me."

Donna blew her a kiss and disappeared into the other room. Reaching for a tissue for the second time in five minutes, Sandra once again wiped at her eyes. She could hear her mother's excitement as she told Maggie what the plans were for the next evening and heard them chatter until the front door closed behind them.

Even with the conflicting emotions swirling through her system, Sandra felt better than she had in days. A positive energy had recharged her and at that moment in time she believed anything was possible. She continued to smile as she replayed her mom's comments and returned her attention to her paperwork.

"What the hell are you thinking?"

No need to see whom the snorting bull in the doorway was. "Go away, Walker, I'm busy."

"You are not going to a community dance tomorrow night."

She refused to let him take away her contentment. Taking a deep breath, she lay her pen down as he commanded the chair in front of her desk.

"I am going to go to the dance and I'm taking my mother. She is looking forward to it as I have been for the past two months. She is, this very moment, heading to the mall to buy something spectacular for the dance. I refuse to disappoint her."

His presence took up the whole room and she had no doubt he was well aware of it. However, she refused to give in to the need to put more physical distance between them than what the desk provided. She was done with backing down. This was her life to live and if she wasn't going to allow Mark to run it then she wasn't going to let Trey Walker run it either.

"It's a dangerous situation. There'll be too many people and Logan and I will have a difficult time keeping track of you."

"Oh, Walker, I didn't realize how much you cared." Sandra placed a hand over her heart. "I'll make sure I leave room on my dance card for you."

"Damn it, Johnson, this isn't funny. Franklin may already be in town and being the snake he has shown himself to be, he'll stop at nothing to get to you, including using the crowd to separate you from us."

There was that tick again by his right eye and Sandra wondered once again if she may have pushed him too far. But then she realized she didn't really care.

"Walker, think about this. If he tried to approach me, I would know. And the crowd is a perfect place to be for safety. I'll be among people I know and trust. They may not know exactly what is happening, but if I am in any danger they will certainly jump in and help."

———

TREY EXHALED and studied her for a moment. Something had changed in the last ten minutes. Over the past few days, he had been with a woman who had vacillated between hiding behind anger and calm. The woman in front of him no longer showed fear. She appeared to be more determined, strong willed and sure of herself more than ever.

His gut instincts were screaming that the dance wasn't a good idea. Not even her explanation, which under normal circumstances would have been sound and logical, could ease the hard knot in his stomach.

Mark Franklin was a slimy snake that had managed to slither his way under the radar of some of the best-trained men and women in the country. Three days into his escape, and they just now had a solid lead.

As much as Trey wanted to believe that Franklin had been close to Ferry City yesterday simply because he was heading to Mexico, he knew better. If Franklin had wanted to go directly to Mexico, he would have been there already. His recent location, instead, spoke volumes that he had taken a route to throw the agency off his trail. Men like Franklin had to feed their ego. They fed off the vulnerabilities of others.

Leaning forward, he placed his arms on her desk. He kept his tone in check as he tried once again to appeal to Sandra's sense of reasoning.

"I appreciate what you've been through with this guy and I won't even pretend I know what you are feeling. I want you to take a moment and think about your mom and dad. If anything happened to you, they would be devastated. I've seen it, Sandra. I've had to be the one to tell families they've lost a loved one. I don't want to have to tell another family, and I certainly don't want to tell your family."

Her eyes darkened as she frowned. This was what he was trained for. Whether in hostage negotiations or in convincing his peers to do things his way, Trey Walker had a way of convincing people to follow his lead.

Trey watched carefully as she seemed to weigh his words. Knowing how she put others before herself, he silently patted himself on the back as he waited patiently for her to accede to his request.

His heart suddenly kicked in his chest causing him to suck in a quick breath as an emotion he hadn't experienced in years exploded and left him feeling helpless. Helpless as doubt nibbled at him. He almost never doubted his abilities, but a vision of Sandra getting hurt made him wonder if he could fulfill his duty to protect her. The idea that he might not be able to protect her scared him. He never got scared.

He had done the unthinkable. He had become emotionally involved. Even though he had kept pushing those feelings away, they kept surfacing at odd moments. Whether she was smiling or arguing with him, the attraction would hit him out of nowhere.

This time, though, it was apparent it was beyond a simple attraction. There was more. He wanted more.

"You know, Walker," Sandra shook her head and he waited for her to tell him how he was right. "I understand what you are trying to do, but it won't work. I refuse to let anyone determine what I can and can't do, including you."

Anger replaced his previous thoughts and he thought about physically restraining her to keep her safe. A picture of carrying her to the car, dragging her into her house and tying her to a bed sprang to mind. However, that image only led him to envisioning her naked and tied to the bed and the feeling of needing her came rushing back to the forefront.

The physical need he felt for her was overwhelming. The emotional need he felt was confusing. However, this was neither the time nor place. His first priority was to protect her, not to seduce her.

"Then at least think of your family. How would your parents feel if something happened to you?"

"I know exactly how they would feel. Been there, done that, remember?"

"Yes, but you didn't die."

"But they believed I was going to. I was on the edge of death and they grieved during that time." She stood and walked around the desk to face him, placing her hands on her hips. "I'm going to go to the dance as I planned. If Mark isn't caught by then, I promise that you can attach me directly to your hip, if need be, but I am going to go enjoy this time with my Mom."

That wasn't even close to ideal in his mind. Perhaps tying her to the bed wasn't a bad idea.

The image of her tied helpless and naked to her bed in anticipation of his touch continued to be a strong vision.

Somehow he had let this woman wriggle her way into his heart and he was willing to do anything to keep her safe. His attraction to her to had become personal and he was having a difficult time keeping the assignment at a consistently professional level. Without saying a word, he walked out of her office. He had to think and reassess. He stood in front of the picture windows of the center and stared into the street, vaguely aware of the cars and people.

His job had always been about protecting clients. He had even taken a bullet for one, superficial as the injury was, but a bullet nonetheless. In his entire time as a Marshal, he had always known death was a possibility. Every agent knew an assignment could end in death for the agent. But it had never dawned on him that he would actually prefer to be the one to die.

He watched Sandra walk to Lacy's desk. Dressed in some kind of yoga apparel, she was the epitome of fit and healthy. The pants hugged her toned legs and butt and the sleeveless top emphasized her lightly muscled upper body. Her hair was tied up into a messy knot on her head, a chaos of loose ends. For a moment he envisioned waking up with this woman. Liquid warmth spilled through his gut and spread throughout his limbs, as the thought of how a warm, sleepy Sandra would feel wrapped in his arms.

He recalled holding her when she had the nightmare that first night. She had been soft and had fit perfectly against him. Her hair had smelled of peaches and he remembered how, while rubbing her back, he had thought he could have done that all night,

He returned to studying the street. From the instant he had met her, he had been attracted. Nothing unusual, really. Any red-blooded male would find her attracted. That hadn't been the first time he had found a client attractive, but always before, he had kept his distance and had never engaged in the cat-and-mouse game Sandra and he seemed to be playing. When had the feelings changed from client to something more personal? That first night in her bedroom?

Trey had certainly gained a new appreciation for Sandra and what she had been through. She acted tough, but that night she had shown her vulnerability. He knew there was a fragility she tried to hide. He admired her determination. Most people would be content to hole up in their environment and wait for the coast-is-clear call to come through before they resumed their lives.

He had to refocus on the assignment. There would be time enough after Franklin was caught to examine what was going on between Sandra and him, if anything. For now he needed to steel himself from any emotional connection with this case. Taking a few slow deep breaths he managed to regroup and push his personal feelings to the back of his mind. Now back to business.

Chapter 14

Sandra was aware of Trey by the windows and knew he had watched her as she walked out of her office and to Lacy. Her nerves were stretched to the max and she hoped they didn't show. The waiting on top of her attraction to Trey was exhausting.

She had been battling anxiety constantly since the Marshals had shown up and it was everything she could do to manage to choke food down. This had to be over soon. The last three days had seemed like three months. Every minute that went by seemed slow and drawn-out.

Danny seemed different now. Ever since the incident with the car that had backfired, he no longer seemed distracted. He was at the top of his game. She hadn't heard Trey upset with him once since that moment. Although Danny still hung around Lacy, he did so by standing between her and the front door. His stance was protective and seemed to stem from the natural instinct males had to protect females.

As much as she wished Trey felt the same toward her, she knew every word he spoke and every action he took was rooted in his job. Nothing would or could interfere with the priority of work. She should be thankful he was so dedicated. However, a part of her would have appreciated seeing more of his personal side.

There had been glimpses, but the moments hadn't lasted long. He returned to work mode so quickly. Trey obviously had a soft and caring side—that was evident from the first night when he had held her until her panic subsided. A passionate side that had come out when he had kissed her. He was a chameleon who changed when the circumstances called for it, and it was very confusing to her.

This was like putting a jigsaw puzzle together. Thinking about Trey Walker's contrasts and contradictions was giving her a headache.

"Thanks, Lacy, for taking care of this."

"Of course."

Sandra walked back to her office. The last client of the day was due in ten minutes, but she wasn't sure she could manage to do any more paper work in that time frame. Fortunately it could wait until Monday. By then things should be back to normal. She crossed her fingers.

Leaning her elbows on her desk, she closed her eyes and rubbed her temples. The headache would only get worse when Trey discovered they were heading to a spaghetti feed that evening. The fact that the event benefitted a family that needed a heart transplant for their four-year old son probably wouldn't sway him. She hadn't mentioned the benefit before because after the dance blowup, she hadn't had the energy to throw down another gauntlet. The only saving grace might be that they would be seated most of the time. Maybe she wouldn't tell Trey until she was ready to head out. That might work. She reached into the top drawer for her bottle of aspirin and took two.

Sandra's last client of the day was Wendy Crosby. Wendy was

a woman in her early forties who had the body of a thirty-year old and loved to flaunt her assets. With the guys in the studio, it only encouraged her to be outrageous more than normal. Who knew weight lifting could be so sensual? With each exaggerated movement, Wendy emphasized body parts that weren't necessarily the focus of the weight group.

Sandra became irritated with Trey as Wendy continuously engaged him in flirtatious conversation. He responded to her as he had with Sandra's friends, but didn't hide the fact that he was eyeing Wendy. He certainly wasn't checking for hidden weapons. In her body-hugging outfit, you could almost make out the shape of her kidneys.

Trey hadn't glanced at Sandra once since Wendy walked in. If Sandra stripped naked, he probably wouldn't even notice. Tempting as that might have been, she wasn't quite that daring.

However, Trey seemed to have no problems still surveying the outside. Danny, on the other hand, seemed to have forgotten about the busy street as well as protecting Lacy. He was openly watching Wendy and only looked up when Lacy hit him on the arm and raised her eyebrows. Sandra wished she could do that with Trey. She shouldn't care and she tried brushing the thought off.

The two-year old in her wanted to stamp her foot and demand that he pay attention to her. At this point, she would take having another argument with him.

"So, Trey, are you going to the spaghetti feed tonight?" Wendy was doing the reverse fly with five-pound dumbbells drawing attention to her abundant chest.

"Spaghetti feed?" Trey's attention quickly turned to Sandra. His eyes narrowed.

"Oh, didn't I tell you, cuz?" Deliberately baiting him, she continued. "I guess it slipped my mind. Now you know. We're going to a spaghetti feed tonight." The last she said with a smile on her face and a shrug of her shoulders. "You don't have a problem with that do you?"

She couldn't help antagonizing him. There was a part of her that wanted to see how far she could poke him until he growled or killed her. However, with an audience she knew she would be safe for now, which made digging at him that much more pleasurable. Later that evening might be another matter.

"I wish you had told me earlier, *cuz*." His response hissed through gritted teeth. "I would have preferred doing something a little more low-key tonight."

"You'll love it. Lots of people, good food and loads of women to flirt with." Sandra continued to smile. "We'll be sure and save you a seat, Wendy."

As much as Trey seemed to like flirting, she knew that the facade would be taxing to maintain for a several hours. Wendy lit up like a Christmas tree and winked at Trey.

"Plus, the feed is for a good cause," Sandra added.

"Perhaps we can discuss this later at home."

"Oh, I wish we could, but the feed starts at 6:00 so we have to go there directly after I close." Her smile grew when she saw him touch the corner of his left eye.

"I think it sounds great. Lacy, are you going?" Danny had been serious and quiet for most of the day. The idea of the spaghetti feed had let loose his inner puppy. He waited expectantly for Lacy's answer.

"Of course, the whole town will probably be there."

Sandra heard what sounded like a groan from Trey's vicinity.

Wendy had one knee on a bench and one foot on the floor doing triceps, her butt perfectly positioned for attention. Neither man was paying attention any longer, as both had moved on. Danny and Lacy continued their conversation while Trey was no doubt plotting ways to kill Sandra. Probably something slow and tortuous.

At five-thirty, Wendy's session was finished. For her final show, she slowly dried the sweat from her neck and chest before seductively dipping the towel into her cleavage. She couldn't have been more obvious in trying to draw Trey's attention again. But it was to no avail, as far as Sandra could tell.

As Wendy said goodbye, Trey finally turned long enough to respond politely. That was the first time Sandra had ever seen Wendy look rejected. She almost felt sorry for her. Almost. No need to worry, as she was sure Wendy would be back in full swing by the time she appeared at the spaghetti feed, much to the chagrin of the other women who were constantly reprimanding their spouses or boyfriends to keep their eyes to themselves. Remembering how Trey had responded to Wendy, she now understood how those women felt.

"We are not going to this wing-ding tonight."

Sandra shrugged. "You may not be, but I am." She continued to wipe down the equipment.

"No, you aren't."

She turned, only to take a step back when she discovered how close he was. A piece of equipment prevented her from backing away further. When she looked, she saw his familiar scowl, but his eyes didn't reflect the anger she thought would be there. She saw something else. Was he truly concerned about her as a person? More than just a part of his job? The look was gone in a snap, replaced by his usual serious look.

She pushed past him and headed to the laundry room, only to have him follow.

"I'm going to the feed, Walker, which means you don't have any choice in the matter."

He grabbed her arm turning her to face him, pulling her close enough to touch. Her first instinct had been to put her hands up against his chest to avoid contact, but she quickly realized that she didn't dare touch him. Even without the contact, heat radiated from him and his scent was earthy and dangerous.

"You're hurting me, Walker." She intentionally glared at the hand gripping her arm. He slowly released his grip.

Sandra turned to finish organizing the laundry for the next day. A sigh escaped her when she heard Trey leave the room and her hands started to shake.

Finished with the towels, she returned to her office and changed into a blouse and a pair of skinny jeans, finishing the outfit off with knee-high boots.

Trey hadn't bothered her since their confrontation. But his presence had kept her on edge, expecting him to blow. She closed her office door and found Danny waiting for her at the front door.

"Where's Walker?"

"He's waiting by the car, keeping an eye on the outside."

Danny exited the building first with Sandra following him. This process had become routine in such a brief time. However, as she approached the side door for her usual seat, Trey opened the passenger door for her instead.

"You're in the front?"

"Why?"

"So you can give me directions to the feed."

"I can do that from the back seat."

Trey didn't respond, but his face spoke volumes. He wasn't going to budge and even in the short period of time she had known him, she knew better than to push him any further. It was apparent that the stunt she had pulled in the studio was still not sitting well with him.

"Okay then."

Climbing into the front seat as he had asked, she settled in and buckled up while he walked around to the driver's side.

From the back seat, Danny spoke up. "Boss, I told Lacy we'd pick her up. Hope that's okay."

Although Sandra couldn't see the left side of his face, she knew the tick was back as he lifted his hand to press a finger against his temple. Pressing her lips together, she turned to view the town and tried her best to keep from smiling. She felt a little relief that Danny had taken Trey's attention away from her and she managed to relax a little.

"Does no one think to ask before hand anymore?" Trey muttered the rhetorical question under his breath as he started the engine.

"What was that, Walker?"

He glanced over at her, his dark eyes showing no mercy. "I need directions to Lacy's."

She noticed he was back to gritting his teeth.

"Thanks, Boss."

Sandra had to bite her lower lip to keep from laughing. She gave him instructions to both Lacy's and the feed. If she had to pay for this later, then so be it. For now, she would enjoy the moment. That was one thing she had learned—how important it was to live for the present.

By the time they arrived at the feed, parking was almost impossible. They were going to have to hoof it for a few blocks. This time Trey's mutterings were of the four-letter kind. Sandra coughed to keep from chuckling as she hung back behind him, but in front of Lacy and Danny.

The line was long and slow. Sandra was afraid Trey was going to explode and bring out the guns to gain access to the front of the line.

"You're going to have a stroke, Walker, if you don't breathe soon."

"Funny, Johnson."

"Come on, lighten up. You need to relax."

Sandra was startled when he turned ever so slightly, hooked her arm and brought her flush up next to him. The action was subtle so as not to draw attention. His stormy face made her realize she might have poked the bear too much.

"If we weren't in a public place, I would turn you over my knee and spank you right here and now."

The image he evoked turned the temperature up in Sandra's abdomen. Her breath caught as he leaned into her and continued in a low voice.

"I'm not here on vacation, Johnson, I'm here to protect your ass. My job is to keep you from harm and when you continuously throw these public appearances into the mix, I'm not going to be happy, so don't expect anything more."

Blinking a few times, Sandra took a few seconds to regroup and tame her physical reaction. He was too close and smelled too good. Behind the intensity of his eyes, Sandra knew, blazed heart and soul, character and life. He was a man's man and women couldn't help but be drawn to him.

"I understand perfectly why you are here, Walker. If you will also remember, I made it clear I wasn't going to stop living my life because the government allowed some nut job to walk out of prison. I've done everything else you requested, so get over yourself."

A part of her knew she was being unreasonable. She could have very well have skipped the feed since she had already donated money, but prodding him made her feel alive. The need to stir things up brought out a passion in both of them. A passion that momentarily took her mind off why he was here.

This was a standoff, pure and simple. Neither was going to budge. The tick in his left eye hadn't let up and now a vein stood out ever so slightly on his forehead as he tightened his grip on her arm.

"Seriously, Walker, you're going to have a stroke and then you'll be no good to me."

The line was moving again and they took a few steps forward. Trey was no longer fixated on her, once again performing his survey routine, jaw clenched, working the muscles overtime. He had relinquished her upper arm only to grab her hand, knowing she wouldn't cause a scene by trying to break away from him.

Trey's height gave him the advantage he needed to view people, but that also gave others an opportunity to see him. Wendy wove her way up to where they were standing. Sandra had to step back or be stepped on as Wendy took up a position inches from Trey's chest. Her breasts were large on any given day, but they now appeared to have grown since Sandra had seen her at the studio.

Sandra tilted her head first to one side then to the other trying to determine if there were tubes attached somewhere that Wendy could pump or blow into at will, as you would a life vest from an airline. Perhaps there were straps she simply pulled on. Not seeing any, Sandra decided the bra Wendy was wearing was either enhanced with gel packs or some duct tape was being used effectively.

"Hey, Trey." Wendy drawled his name out, slow and seductive, and then licked her lips in the same slow, seductive manner in which she had spoken.

Sandra raised her eyebrows.

"Hi, Wendy." Trey only glanced at her.

But that was all the invitation Wendy needed. She thrust her breasts against Trey's arm. His eyes dropped to her chest and then back to her eyes.

As if Sandra wasn't even present, or anyone else for that matter, Wendy purred in a mere whisper, "Do you like what you see?"

"I suppose they're okay if you're into those kinds of things."

Wendy's eyes grew big and she moved back a little. The pseudo-innocence had disappeared and pure bewilderment showed on her face.

"I don't think I understand."

"I'm not into boobs." Trey shrugged his shoulders as if that answered everything clearly.

Sandra took a step behind him so Wendy couldn't see her hold her hand over her mouth in order to keep from laughing out loud. She had to give him credit. He was such a macho man that to have others believe he played for the same team took a lot of guts. On the other hand, she supposed that was a nice way to let Wendy down. She peered around Trey's broad shoulders.

"But all guys like breasts." Wendy took hold of hers for emphasis. "Unless..."

Sandra saw the realization dawn slowly on Wendy. "You mean you're...?"

"Yes I am."

Sandra leaned her forehead against his back and covered her mouth once again. She counted slowly to ten in an attempt to take her mind off the ridiculous conversation.

"Oh, I would never have guessed." Wendy took a couple of steps back. "Well, I've got to go. Have a great time."

She waved her fingers at them before darting after a poor unsuspecting guy walking past. Wendy began chatting him up, while the guy looked like he had hit the jackpot. Soon she was wrapping her arm into his, pressing her breasts against him. Sandra finally laughed out loud as the crowd swallowed up the two of them.

"What are you laughing about?"

"Oh, my gosh, I can't believe you had the guts to lead her to believe you were gay. It'll make a great story for her."

"I didn't say anything about being gay."

"You implied you were gay by saying you weren't into breasts."

"I'm not into breasts."

She turned in surprised.

"Don't give me that shit. Every guy is into breasts and not for one minute do I believe you're gay." Although for just a moment, the thought had tickled her mind.

"I'm not gay nor am I into breasts." Trey continued to scan the crowd as he continued. "I'm a leg and butt guy. I can't help it if she took my comment as something else."

"Oh." She mentally kicked herself for having the slightest doubt about his sexuality. His kisses had been proof of that. "Not into breasts, though, huh?"

He turned and pointedly looked down at her firm but normal-sized breasts. Sandra felt the blush creeping up her neck to her face. Her pulse jumped.

Trey's eyes traveled slowly from her chest to her neck and back to her eyes. The heat deepened in her face and her breath became ragged. The areas his eyes had landed on felt as if he had physically touched her

"Legs and butt."

He leaned forward, his breath but a whisper on her neck. She felt herself sway towards him so she didn't miss what he had to tell her. Or so she told herself. She was desperate to feel skin-on-skin.

"And you have both in spades."

Sandra was afraid to move. The soft caress of his words brushed her neck, causing goose bumps. Just as quickly he shifted away, back to his Marshal mode.

Sandra suddenly felt the need for a cold shower. Her skin was heated, her knees weak and her imagination was working overtime as she thought of Trey satisfying her as only a man could satisfy a woman.

She lifted her hair from the nape of her neck, hoping for a cool breeze, wishing she had something to fan the heat from her face. How pathetic to respond like that to a man she had barely known for four days.

Sandra remained behind Trey as they made their way to the front of the line in hopes the heat would die down and her coloring would return to normal. At the very least, close to normal. This madness with Trey Walker needed to be over soon. Where was that damn phone call saying they had captured Mark?

Chapter 15

Although the spring days had been warm, the evenings proved to be cool. Mark Franklin was appreciative of the light jacket he had thought to bring with him as he perched in the tree above Sandra's backyard.

Mark enjoyed a view of the street, but his vantage point only included a portion of the black top. He would have to rely on the lights going on in the house for him to know when she returned to the house.

The tree foliage was thick and for someone to see him, they would have to climb up a few branches. He kept glancing at his watch. He had expected Sandra to have come home well before now, since she closed her business at five-thirty on Fridays. It was pushing eight-thirty and he found himself growing impatient. He wanted to finish what he'd come to do and get the hell out of the states.

He took a deep breath and reminded himself that waiting a little longer wouldn't make a difference.

The sound of a vehicle coming down the street caught his attention. He hoped it wasn't yet another neighbor coming home. Mark saw the headlights reflected on the street and could tell the car was slowing down. The headlights pulled to the right and he could see the front of the SUV as it came to a stop in front of the house.

Mark caught a glimpse of the big guy rounding the front of the SUV. It didn't take long before the lights came on inside the house, as well as the back porch light.

He made a mental note that he would have to unscrew the bulb if she were in the habit of leaving the porch light on all night. A spotlight was not what he needed when he broke in.

The slider opened and he swore under his breath. The biggest dog he had ever seen came bounding out, making a beeline for the tree he was in, barking loudly. Mark glanced around at the other houses half expecting porch lights to turn on and people gathering to see what the dog was barking at.

"Tiny, leave the squirrel alone and get the job done."

Barking once more, the dog lifted his leg and peed on the tree, glancing up again before trotting off. Once the dog was safely inside, Franklin let out the breath he had been holding. Damn it, now he had to think about a freaking dog. He contemplated how to handle this new hurdle.

The night was dark enough for him to leave the tree without being seen. Mark retreated to his car and drove to the nearest grocery store where he grabbed some packaged lunchmeat and some cold medicine.

He returned to Sandra's house and the tree. As he suspected, the dog was put outside again and immediately started barking at him. Mark dropped a packet of lunchmeat with the cold medicine inside. The dog stopped barking long enough to wolf it down. Mark dropped another, and then another until the dog had ingested enough to either sleep for several hours or die. Either way, he didn't care.

Ten minutes later the dog was back inside. The kitchen lights were doused as well as the porch light. Then Sandra's bedroom and bathroom lights came on. Mark waited for the bodyguards to leave, but their SUV remained parked.

Another hurdle to ponder, but nothing he couldn't figure out. He highly doubted she would share her bedroom with either of the men and he knew she preferred the door to her bedroom closed. Even if the dog slept in her room, by midnight he'd be sound asleep.

Pleased with himself for navigating the bumps in the road, Mark imagined the horror on her face when she saw him. He knew that seeing him again was her greatest fear. He couldn't wait to see the panic in her eyes. It would almost be worth the years he had lost because of her.

He settled into as comfortable a position as any person could in a tree. The sound of an occasional car in the distance and the occasional barking of a dog were the only things that broke the silence of the night. Other neighboring lights were slowly doused. It was pushing eleven so he knew her lights would go out soon.

A light suddenly came on in the kitchen and the sider was shoved aside. Staying perfectly still, Mark watched as first the dog then Sandra came rushing through the door followed by the large bodyguard.

Damn it! That dog should be passed out in a corner somewhere. What the hell was going on?

"I don't know what's wrong with him." Sandra squatted down next to Tiny and rubbed and patted his back as he heaved up more of his dinner. The first mess he had made was in the middle of her bedroom floor.

She squinted up at Trey and Danny as they joined her. Danny was rubbing his eyes and yawning while Trey appeared wide awake. He briefly surveyed the yard before turning his attention back to her. He crouched down on the other side of Tiny and also rubbed his back.

"Has he done this before?"

"Never. He must have gotten into something."

Both of them turned simultaneously to Danny. He was stretching, oblivious to their attention. Finally he noticed them.

"What?"

"Did you by any chance give the dog something extra to eat tonight?"

"No, why would I do that?"

"Cause I've seen you feed him from your plate."

"Well, yeah, I've done that before."

"Did you happen to give him any of your supply of chocolate?"

Danny squirmed a little. "Not on purpose. I turned my back for a second and half of the chocolate bar was gone."

"You mean half of one of those king-size bars? Danny, dogs shouldn't have chocolate, that can kill them." Sandra returned her attention to Tiny.

Tiny had given up on standing, but seemed to be feeling better after upchucking everything. His tail was slowly thumping the ground as Sandra talked softly.

"I'm sorry, Sandra. I didn't even realize he was close by when I put the bar down."

Trey ran his hand through his hair and muttered something under his breath. "How do you miss a hundred pound dog, Logan? He takes up the whole damn house, for God's sake."

"Sorry, Boss, sorry, Sandra. Really."

"He didn't give him chocolate intentionally, Walker, and Tiny doesn't seem worse for the wear." She coaxed Tiny to stand. "Come on boy, I think we're safe to return to the house."

Tiny slowly padded behind her and headed straight for his water. He only took a few laps of water before heading back to her bedroom.

Trey was the last to enter the house, locking the slider and putting the metal bar back in its place.

"I have to clean up the mess in my room, but you guys go on back to bed."

"Logan will help you." He gave Danny a measured look that didn't allow him to respond any other way but in the affirmative.

―――――

WHAT THE HELL?

If only Mark had his gun. He would have taken all three of them out, if for no other reason than the lanky guy screwing up his plans. How could someone who didn't seem to have an ounce of common sense be so lucky? Obviously the dog had thrown up everything he had ingested, including the pills.

For good measure he may have to take the Logan guy out as well as the Walker guy. He softly chuckled at the thought of how the government would react to three deaths rather than one.

Waiting a while longer to make sure no one would be coming back out, Mark jumped to the alley and jogged down the block to his car. He rubbed his hands together, cupped them and blew into them to take the chill off.

As much as he wanted to take care of Sandra in a more private setting, time was becoming a problem. The authorities would catch up with him if he stayed in this place too much longer. He had to take care of this in the next twenty-four hours. Putting the car into gear, he pulled away from the curb, a plan already taking shape.

―――――

EVEN WITH THE little sleep Sandra had managed, she was able to get out of bed in time for a short run with Trey and also to say hello to Mr. Ferguson.

"How are things this morning, Mr. Ferguson?"

"Very well, thank you Sandra." He stopped on the sidewalk as if he had more to say, something he had never done before. "I see you've had company staying with you the last few days."

"Yes, some cousins I hadn't seen in a while." She smiled at him hoping he would believe her blatant lie and turned to introduce one of her "cousins". "This is Trey Walker. My cousin Danny is inside."

"Nice to meet you, Mr. Ferguson."

"Nice to meet you as well, Mr. Walker." He tipped his hat to Sandra and continued his journey. "Have a nice day."

"You too, Mr. Ferguson." She sipped at her coffee and watched him until he entered his house. "I hate lying."

"It won't be for much longer."

"How many times have you said that to me, Walker? This is getting old. I want results not promises."

Sandra, as usual, couldn't read his expression. She let out a frustrated sigh.

"Well, time for work. Only six hours today and then the big dance."

She was in the "poking the bear" mood. His response was a frown. Without saying a word or even glancing at her, he opened the door and waited for her to enter the house. The only time she really knew what he was thinking or feeling was if he was in a foul mood.

"Do you ever smile? Even if it is just to smile?"

"I smile when there is something to smile about." He turned his gaze to her after locking the door behind them.

"The only time I've seen you smile is when women are flirting like crazy with you."

"Having women flirt with me is something to smile about."

A little spark touched his eyes for a moment, but just as quickly disappeared.

"However, my job is serious business. There's nothing to smile about when you are trying to catch bad guys or preventing people from being killed."

"Well then, tonight shouldn't be too much of a heartache for you. There'll be plenty of women who will flirt with you. That should keep you smiling all night."

Sandra added her own smile. She purposefully had avoided talk about the seriousness of his job. Although encouraging him to flirt wasn't exactly something to be enthusiastic about either. Both subjects balled her stomach up in knots.

"Tonight is business."

"So was a few nights ago when we went to the bar."

He touched the corner of his left eye with his index finger.

"And that's how I conducted it."

"Flirting with all the women and Frank?"

"I was not flirting with Frank."

"Kissing me?"

He shoved his hands through his impossibly thick hair leaving a few strands to stand on end while the rest fell right back into place. Her fingers itched to smooth the strays into place. To keep from acting on the thought, she balled her hands into fists as he muttered under his breath which Sandra was sure not pretty language.

"This conversation is over. Grab your stuff so we can leave."

As she headed to her bedroom to brush her teeth she couldn't help but add, "I'm just saying you should wear something pretty tonight. Frank likes flashy."

Smiling to herself, she didn't bother to turn and see his reaction since he had once again taken to muttering under his breath.

At Sandra's business, the day wasn't especially full so the

unscheduled pockets of time could be spent on paperwork. As it turned out, though, the paperwork would have to wait while she returned several messages from single women, including Wendy, who wanted to schedule time for a workout. Obviously the word had spread that her "cousin" hung out at the studio with her. Apparently the idea that Trey might be gay hadn't deterred Wendy from trying again.

Sandra filled the empty spots. She purposefully filled them with single women whose physical assets were not as pronounced as Wendy's. Two were women in their late sixties who had never worked out with Sandra. She only knew them through the work she did at the community center.

Her phone call to Wendy was apologetic as she explained that the schedule was full for the day, but that she'd see her at her regular time the following week. Before the conversation was over, though, Wendy asked if she and her cousins were going to the dance. Not being able to lie her way out of that one, Sandra had to concede that they were. She stared at the phone for a second, a little ashamed of manipulating the matter.

The fact she had been so purposeful in choosing who could ogle Trey and vice-versa had her cheeks heating up. She placed her hands on her face in an attempt to cool down as she came to grips with her true motive.

Watching Wendy flaunt herself at Trey had set off the green monster in the pit of Sandra's stomach. She had no claim on him and she wasn't even sure she liked him.

Except for his kisses and the breath of his whisper on her neck and the smoldering of passion in her belly whenever he came near her. The heat never seemed to leave her now, so the moment he was inches from her, flames raged out of control.

The lack of physical contact she had had with men in the past three years obviously wasn't cutting it. That was the best excuse she could come up with as to why she kept having such a physical reaction to Trey.

To admit she liked him wasn't even on her radar. That couldn't be possible. He was irritating, full of himself and a ladies' man. Any minute now he would receive a phone call saying to wrap the case up and he would jet off to rescue the next person.

Sandra shoved her chair from the desk perhaps a little too hard and exited her office to check on the towels. She transferred the wet towels to the dryer and proceeded to set up the equipment for her first client, deliberately filling her head with business.

She refused to give any of her attention to Trey Walker as he made himself at home with his laptop in the front of the studio, watching the street. Danny was once again standing guard over Lacy, his attention focused on the street as well. Although this wasn't Lacy's normal day to come in, she had made up some excuse about checking next week's appointments. Sandra was glad she had done so, otherwise there would have been way too much testosterone in the studio and that was just from Trey.

Sandra continued to argue with herself as she pushed her client through her routine. Why, of all the men she had met over the past few years, was Trey Walker the one who had slithered under her skin? It had completely blindsided her.

Perhaps she had been over-thinking this whole thing. But then she'd glance at Trey only to find him watching her. Heat would once again surge to her cheeks as she remembered his kisses and the doubt started the arguments once again in her head.

She had no time during the day to regroup and her clients weren't keeping her mind off Trey so the vicious circle between logic and emotions continued. Sandra's head began to pound.

She choked down a few bites of lunch while Trey, Danny and

Lacy enjoyed the pizza they had ordered. It was completely illogical to feel left out of their circle.

They had offered for her to join them, but she had declined. They carried on such an effortless conversation that she felt like a third wheel. Even her client, Betsey Stranahan, had joined their conversation.

Feeling like an outsider in her own studio, she concentrated fully on Betsey's workout, perhaps pushing her further then necessary in an attempt to punish someone. By the time Betsey left, however, she had managed to extract the promise of a dance from Trey later that evening.

"Something wrong, Sandra?"

Usually so careful with her weights, the two-year old in her was having a fit again and in doing so, wasn't placing the weights back in their proper place without making more noise then necessary. She supposed the argument she was muttering to herself had drawn his attention.

Forcing a bright smile that didn't reach her eyes, she responded. "Things are peachy."

Done with the weight room, she headed to the laundry room to fold towels and ready the dirty towels for a load.

"Come on, Johnson, you're obviously peeved about something. You'll feel better if you say what you want to say."

"Go away, Walker."

She continued folding the towels, but knew he hadn't moved. Without even turning, she knew he would be leaning against the doorjamb studying her. Her hands were shaking from the intensity of emotions she had been grappling with.

Neither one of them said anything as she finished folding the towels. Placing them on the shelves, she braced herself to exit past Trey, praying to avoid physical contact. He had different ideas. Within a few steps of making it out the door, he purposefully blocked her.

"Move, please." She used his gritted teeth technique and stared at his chest. She waited for him to move. When he didn't, she was forced to make eye contact.

"Why are you running, Sandra?"

He spoke her name with such softness. Like he really cared about her answer. His gentleness was almost her undoing. Almost. Somewhere deep within, she dug her pride out to save her.

"I'm not running, Walker. If you must know I'm having my cycle and am fighting a migraine."

Usually a woman mentioning female problems would send a man hoofing it as fast as possible. Apparently Trey was made of sterner stuff.

"Bullshit. I'd say you were jealous."

"Jealous? What in the world would I be jealous of?"

"The women who hit on me."

"I'm surprised you can walk through a door with that swollen ego."

Sandra placed her hand on his chest to push him to one side. He didn't budge. Instead he covered her hand with his imprisoning it on his chest forcing her to feel the beat of his heart. Forcing her to once again look him in the eyes.

They were unreadable. Her surprise at his touch was no doubt written on her face. The beat of his heart sent her pulse on a race of its own. Seconds passed. He finally released her hand and stepped to one side.

Her first step was a little wobbly. By sheer determination she moved by him and made a beeline for her office so she could catch her breath. Breathing a sigh of relief that he hadn't followed her, she placed a hand over her own heart. Her heartbeat was off the charts and she took some deep breaths in an effort to calm herself.

"This is so stupid and crazy. No one should have that kind of response to someone else." She leaned on her desk and closed her eyes waiting for her breathing to normalize. "I'm tired and this headache is making the whole situation worse. This can't go on much longer. He'll be gone soon and then I can laugh at how foolish I've been. And, I need to stop talking to myself."

She readied her desk for the next workday. Her mind no longer seemed to be firing on all cylinders and she could only hope that Monday would be back to normal. No more threats, no more Marshals, a regular Monday. If she wanted it to be a regular Monday, then why did she feel such a sense of loss?

Danny waited by the door for her since Trey was already outside.

Sandra went through the motions of closing her business. The dance was no longer an appealing outing, but others were expecting her and would be concerned if she didn't show. So wrapped up in her revolving emotions, she didn't pay attention to the bustling street as she usually did. The activity of the town gave her a sense of belonging. Because of that, she missed the nondescript white car as it cruised by. Even if she had noticed and had seen the man glance in her direction, the hat pulled low over his eyes was enough to even disguise him from her.

Chapter 16

The hubbub around town was about the community dance that evening. Mark decided to use the get together as his Plan B.

From the conversations at the doughnut shop, he had gathered that the dance was an annual event, drawing many people from neighboring farm communities. Sandra had always enjoyed social functions, so he didn't doubt for a moment that she'd be there.

He knew showing up could prove to be dangerous if anyone recognized him, but the idea of getting caught seemed to only fuel his adrenal rush. Like the idea of being caught in an illicit affair.

When he had cruised past her business Mark had known his idea may not be the best, that the scheme may expose him, but that hadn't fazed him. As he suspected, no one paid a bit of attention to him in the midst of the hustle of the mid-afternoon shopping. Sandra was turning from locking up her studio when he drove by, but her attention was somewhere else.

The big guy was already behind the wheel with his sunglasses pulled over his eyes while the lanky guy opened the back door of the vehicle for Sandra. He glanced in his rearview mirror and watched the young guy climb in and the SUV do a U-turn, heading the opposite direction from him. He smiled and then chuckled. *Yes, Sandra, dear, enjoy your last few hours.*

Not wanting to take a chance on the authorities knowing he was in the town of Ferry City, Mark hadn't bothered to register at a motel. Instead, he had found an empty gravel pit outside of town where he could easily hide the car. He had spent the night there sleeping beneath the stars.

The dance was still several hours away and he didn't want to implement his plan until the dance was well underway. The community center, an old barn with a fresh coat of red paint and white trim, had been busy all day with preparations that had made it impossible for him to scope out the interior of the building.

The double doors had been wide open as people carried tables and chairs inside. There was a small bell tower off to the side of the front door, along with pots of flowers. Everything was oh-so-very cozy. Too bad he wasn't a cozy kind of guy.

Outside the center was a large paved parking lot with additional parking marked off in the surrounding field. They were expecting a lot of people. That would make it easier for him to blend in, since he wouldn't be the only new face.

Arriving back at the gravel pit, he was careful to make sure no other cars were on the country road before turning in and making his way over to the mound of rocks that would hide the car.

The last few days had been nice, but the spring nights were still cold. He parked the car and popped the trunk where he had a satchel of clothes and food and water.

Removing his shirt, he used it to wipe the grime and sweat off his neck and face. Grabbing a fresh pair of jeans and shirt, he changed and felt he would pass fine as a neighboring farmer. He even had a fresh ball cap for good measure.

As much as he had hated wearing cheap, off-the-rack clothes rather than the designer couture he was accustomed to, he needed them in order to fit in. Mark ran his hand over the scruff of the beard that had grown over the last several days. It had come in quite gray and was a nice addition for the appearance of a neighboring farmer rather than an influential stockbroker.

This was it. Finally he was going be rid of the woman who had cost him so much. The wait had been worth it.

"Mom, what are you doing here? I thought we were going to meet at the dance."

"I couldn't wait to show you what I bought." Taking off the cream-colored trench coat, Donna proceeded to spin with her arms open to make sure they saw everything.

She was wearing a neon pink blouse tucked into a pair of black jeans with a studded rhinestone belt and designer cowboy boots.

"Wow, Mom."

Sandra was stunned. Her mom normally liked understated items. Maggie had obviously been an influence on their shopping spree. Sandra wondered if Donna would ever find another event to wear the outfit to.

"Umm.... err.... I'll be able to pick you out of the crowd."

"What? You don't like it?"

"Actually I do like it. It suits you. I bet your dance card will fill fast. Not sure how Dad's going to feel about that, though."

"Oh, posh. Your Dad has nothing to worry about." Donna couldn't help but smile. "Look at Maggie."

Taking off her coat, Maggie stunned everyone when they saw she was wearing a loose fitting animal print top that hit her at mid-thigh and was paired with black leggings. Instead of her typical four-inch heels, she wore a pair of gladiator sandals with a slight wedge and decorated with crystals.

"Oh, Maggie, you look beautiful."

"Thank you."

Sandra had never seen Maggie blush before and would never have thought that possible. For as long as she had known the woman, she had always worn tight-fitting clothes. She now wondered if Maggie had thought body-hugging clothing was the most attractive on her. She hoped this version of Maggie would become the new normal.

Danny gave a whistle. "Man, Maggie and Donna, you gals will be the hit of the dance. I hope you will both do me the honor of saving me a dance."

They responded in unison, "We'd love it."

Everyone looked at Trey expectantly. "What?" He was still grumpy. No one said a word as he eyed each of them. "I don't dance."

"You're such a kill-joy, Walker."

Sandra went to let Tiny out one last time before they left. She stepped out with him, basking in the cool air. Just being in the vicinity of Trey managed to heat her up faster than an electric blanket.

When the slider opened behind her, she expected to see her mother. Instead Trey joined her. She had hoped she wouldn't have to have any more alone time with him. From the moment they had met she had been drawn to him, physically at least. And it hadn't stopped there. She had seen his softer side and was attracted to his intelligence as well as his sense of duty and commitment.

"Tiny, come on boy, time to go inside."

Not wanting to be alone for any length of time with Trey, she clapped and called to Tiny to hurry him along. He came running and Trey slid the door open for him, closed the access as Sandra tried to follow him inside.

"We better go, Walker."

"Am I making you uncomfortable?"

"No." She stared at the pulse beating at the base of his neck, avoiding his eyes. She stepped to one side to gain access to the door as well as to get some breathing space. He blocked her immediately, forcing her to finally look up at him. Warmth spread through her limbs and she felt lightheaded.

"I want you to reconsider going tonight."

She shook her head. "I can't let someone determine where I can go and what I can do, especially Mark. My whole life was changed because of him. Besides the months of my physical recovery, I had to also go through a mental recovery. You don't understand how overwhelming those days were."

"You're right, I don't. What I do know is what is here and now. As confident as we are in our ability to protect you, it becomes more problematic when you add a sea of people."

Closing her eyes, Sandra rubbed her temples wishing for the pounding of the "what ifs" to go away. Taking a deep breath proved to be a mistake when she smelled his cologne. Her stomach once again churned with a desire to touch him.

He was going to be gone soon. Trey could be gone in an hour or tomorrow. The agency was closing in on Mark and the one man she had come to trust and feel close to, despite his by-the-book attitude and lack of patience, would be leaving soon.

Perhaps it was because she had known the situation was short-term she had given herself time to test the waters a little. Trey was an attractive man who had shown an interest in her. Who could possibly resist feeling something? From the beginning, she knew there hadn't been a chance for them to have a permanent relationship so it only made sense to take the opportunity to play a little. Right?

Oh, who was she kidding? Who wouldn't want to hit that? If

they lived in the same town, she would probably be stalking him and would appear as needy as all the other single women. And Frank.

Maybe that was all this was. She needed some good sex. As much as she wanted to believe that theory, she knew better. She had never been the type of girl to have a fling just for sexual benefits. She needed that emotional connection between a man and woman.

In a few short days, Trey had shown more concern about her well being than Mark had the entire time they had been together. Even with the knowledge that taking care of her was Trey's job, he hadn't been as immune to her as he wanted her to think.

Now he took her by her forearms and pulled her against him. "I lost a partner while doing my job and that tore my gut out. That was one too many. So you need to listen to me and listen carefully."

There was no breathing space, no way for oxygen to fill her lungs. The heat between them and the lack of air was causing her limbs to weaken.

His eyes bore into hers and the intensity scared her. The heat that was ever present when they were near each other and the lack of air was causing her limbs to weaken.

"You will be glued to my side all evening, do you understand? The only time we are separated is when you use the restroom, and even then there will only be a door between us."

His gaze dropped to her lips. They were parted as she struggled to find air. When he looked into her eyes she knew her emotions were on full display.

"You will not go off with your friends or your mother without me. Do you understand?" Trey's voice was a whisper on her lips.

She could only nod. If she had spoken, she was sure her

words would have been incoherent. For a moment, she wondered if he was going to kiss her. One more kiss, just one more before he left. One more that she could burn into her memory. A kiss that meant something and wasn't just a passing fancy.

"Come on you guys, the dance will be in full swing by the time we get there and I don't want to miss out on the fun."

Donna couldn't see her around Trey's broad back. Sandra's disappointment quickly replaced the desire burning in the pit of her stomach as Trey released her and turned, blocking her mom from viewing her just yet. She was thankful for the time to gather some composure.

"Okay then, let's go."

He stepped into the kitchen moving to one side for Sandra to follow before securing the slider. As she left the kitchen she heard her mom ask Trey what they had been doing.

"Making sure we were on the same page for security purposes."

The SUV was large enough for all of them to pile in, effectively eliminating an extra car to worry about parking at the center. The year prior had been Sandra's first experience of the annual dance so she knew the turnout would be great.

She was thankful for the twenty-minute drive so she had time to recover somewhat from the emotions she experienced on the deck. Those moments had confirmed for her how she felt about Trey. She had fallen in love. Fallen in love with an unattainable man. He was hours from turning his back on yet another finished job and sadness settled into her bones.

Once parked, each of them exited the vehicle helped either by Danny or Trey. When Trey extended his hand to help Sandra, she accepted only long enough for her feet to hit solid ground. She stepped away from him, falling into place with the others as they headed towards the music and noise of the dance in full swing. The moment was short-lived as he fell into step next to her.

"Remember. You promised." He said the words so only she could hear.

How could she forget? Her arms were still warm from where he had gripped them and the smell of his cologne was etched into her senses. As much as she wished he didn't have to leave, the sooner he did the sooner she could have her life back. Her life hadn't been that bad. Perhaps somewhat lonely at times. Girlfriends were wonderful and dependable, but having a man around to spend time with had brought back the desire to share her life experiences with someone. Tears stung the back of Sandra's eyes and she blinked several times.

Digging deep, she managed to put a sincere smile on her face as they entered the community center. The gravel path leading to the large double doors had been lit with tiki torches and potted plants. The open double doors were outlined in Christmas lights and overhead lights dimly lighted the interior. Candle sconces lined the walls.

The dance floor was full with young and old. High barista tables were scattered near the walls for people to stand at and talk. A bar was set up to the right of the doors and Sandra knew a second bar had been set up in one of the back corners.

In no time, she was introducing her friends to her mother and Maggie. The husbands of the few who were married were introduced to Trey and Danny.

Now that Sandra was among her friends, she felt her earlier tension slip away. Tonight would be fun. She was determined the dance would be especially fun for her mom.

"Mom and Maggie, do you want a drink? I'm buying." A shot of courage seemed to be in order tonight.

"Definitely."

Hooking her arm through Donna's, Sandra led the group

over to the bar. Her single girlfriends followed, vying to engage Trey in conversation. She had to give him credit. He could have been a jerk to them, but he made small talk with each. By the end of the evening, there was a good chance there could be a catfight over him.

"Hey, Billy, how are doing?" Sandra leaned her elbows on the bar so she could be heard over the noise. "This is my Mom, Donna, and her friend Maggie."

———

BILLY SMILED at Sandra and said hi to Donna and Maggie. Trey immediately disliked him. He was young and had the boy-next-door look, flicking thick blond hair out of his eyes with a shake of his head. Billy's shoulders were broad and Trey guessed he had probably been a football player. He moved closer to Sandra. For a second he forgot that he was here doing a job.

"Man, I can tell where your looks came from, Sandra." Billy kissed Donna's hand.

Not wanting to be left out, Maggie extended hers as well. "What can I serve you ladies?"

Both Donna and Maggie ordered red wine.

"Give me a shot of your best vodka," Sandra said.

"Hitting it hard tonight, huh?"

Billy placed the shot in front of Sandra and, without hesitation, she swigged the liquor in one gulp. "Hit me again, Billy."

He raised an eyebrow at her, obviously surprised. "Are you sure?"

"Yep, and get my friend whatever he wants." She motioned with her thumb toward Trey. "Billy Jones, meet Trey Walker."

Billy eyed Trey carefully and the testosterone level rose. Trey knew the glare. He was being sized up. The bartender was figuring out how to beat the competition. Trey wanted to assure him he wasn't competition, but knew that would be a lie. The guy was a player and he didn't want Sandra playing with him.

"Just a Coke for now."

"Sure."

Billy placed the soda on the bar and returned his attention to Sandra.

Trey was glad to see she was sipping the second shot. After watching her down the first, he had been sure he was going to have to carry her to the car before the evening was over. Of course, that would have taken care of keeping her in one place and away from danger. He hadn't anticipated that danger would include the likes of a bartender.

"So, Sandra, when are you going to finally say yes to going out with me?"

Obviously feeling braver after her first shot, she glanced at Trey and then gave Billy a smile. "You're right. We should go on a date."

"Great."

Billy smirked at Trey. A simple punch to the face would wipe the smug look right off.

"Come on, Sandra, they're playing our song."

Trey took her glass and placed it on the bar and grabbed her hand leading her onto the dance floor. It was a slow dance and he gathered her in his arms, snug up against him making sure Billy got the message.

"Hey." She tried to push against him for some distance, but he was too strong for her. "We don't have a song."

"We do now." The thought made him smile, especially when he saw the glare Billy was giving him.

"You don't like me enough to want to have a song with me."

"Who says?"

"No one. It's just that it's obvious from the way you treat me."

Trey pulled back to look at the woman who had managed to

capture his full attention from their first meeting. The woman who had irritated him beyond all measure but whom was also the most fascinating woman he had ever met. Tonight he had finally had to admit to himself that Sandra was the woman he had been waiting for. Waiting to get to know better, wanting to spend all of his spare time with and to plan a future with.

"I've treated you as I do every case." Just because he had finally acknowledged to himself that she was the one didn't mean he was ready to spill his guts.

From the start he *had* treated her differently. He had convinced himself that was because she was defiant and stubborn. In his previous cases, everyone had been so grateful to have him there that they not once questioned what was expected of them.

He had finally understood that the defiance was her wall. Her cheekiness was her way of keeping her past at a distance. He couldn't blame her. What had happened to her was unforgivable and she had done an admirable job of moving past the train wreck and creating a new beginning.

But even acknowledging that hadn't stopped him from pushing her. He had found some kind of gratification when she pushed back. Trey liked when she was fired up over something he did or said. He liked her quick-witted responses that made him smile. She was an intelligent, gifted woman whose energy for life made him think beyond a short-term relationship for the first time in his adult life.

Now wasn't the time, however, to pursue this train of thought. He was still on the job and he had already crossed the line by becoming engaged emotionally. Until the job was done, he had to keep his head in the game.

"You must have received glowing reviews from your previous clients then. When this is over, I plan on letting your boss know what a pain-in-the-ass you've been."

"I'm afraid it's a little too late for that." He smiled at her. "She's been getting the same complaint for years."

———

THE SHOT of vodka had warmed Sandra instantly and eventually made her mind a bit fuzzy. She had drunk more liquor in three days than she had in three months. An occasional drink over an entire evening with friends was her limit. Being in the company of Trey Walker apparently led her to drink.

Her single friends were on the edge of the crowd, ready to pounce on Trey as soon as the dance was finished. This made her smile.

If he hadn't kissed her like a man knows how to kiss a woman, she would have figured he was more of Frank's type. The feelings he had aroused in her since the moment they met were confusing. Those feelings of wanting to be with someone had been purposefully pushed down for so long that she had thought she was long past the schoolgirl giddiness.

It wasn't as if her responses to the opposite sex had been dormant. There had been a number of attractive men who had sent her heart racing, but there had been no emotional connection. The connection that makes you want to talk to them all night about anything and everything. The connection that was both physical and intellectual. A connection that involved all the senses.

"What was the sigh for?"

Sandra stepped away from him as the song ended. "I didn't realize I had."

"It was huge." Again, the smile that made her heart beat a little too fast.

"It must have been because I'm surprised you can dance."

She responded sarcastically, not wanting him to know what she had been thinking.

"Were you afraid I would step on your toes?"

"Honestly? Yes. Your big feet could do some damage."

"Now you know. I'm light on my feet."

"Hey, Trey, can I have the next dance?"

Carla had sidled up next to them without either noticing. She rubbed his arm and looked up at him through her eyelashes playing the coy virgin. Sandra gave a disgusted snort before she could stop.

They both glanced at her and Carla seemed surprised Sandra was still standing next to them. Trey smiled as if knowing what Sandra was thinking.

"Sorry." She pursed her lips to keep from smiling. Trey understood her. No guy had understood her like he did.

"As much as I would like to, Carla, I'm already promised out several dances."

Sandra couldn't stop the surprise look she knew crossed her face. When had he had time to promise other dances?

Carla continued to rub his arm slowly. She wasn't deterred, which didn't surprise Sandra. She knew her friend well and Carla was persistent once she set her sights on someone. Most men responded to her immediately, but on occasion she had to work a little harder. Trey Walker was one Carla would have to work harder on. Sandra mentally wished her good luck because she couldn't see him budging.

"When you find a free one, be sure to find me. I won't be far away."

"You will be the first one."

They watched as she walked away in her four-inch heels, hips swaying perfectly to the beat of the music. Carla knew how to work her body. Her walk drew the attention of several men who stopped dancing to watch her walk by. A few of those men were married and were promptly punched in the arm by their wives. Sandra noted that even Frank had stopped, drink in hand, to watch.

"I need another drink." Sandra said with a sigh.

Chapter 17

Sandra headed to the bar. She came up short when Trey took her arm and steered her toward a different part of the building.

"Oh, I think you've had enough." He grabbed her hand, pulling her behind him as they wove their way deeper into the crowd. "You don't exactly strike me as the type who drinks when they're dealing with a problem," he commented over his shoulder.

"The only problem I have is you, Walker, which, coincidently, is when I started drinking more than usual. Hmm, imagine that."

He found a spot behind several fake trees clustered together, which provided a sanctuary of privacy from the throngs of people. As he pulled her in behind him, Sandra discovered there was barely space for the both of them, and the coals of passion lying dormant in her belly flared to life when she found herself with her back against the wall and Trey pressed up against her.

"And you seem to be my problem."

His words sealed the deal. Sandra knew her heart was spoken for. This man had taken her heart and she could no longer avoid her feelings. He had successfully gotten past the barriers she had erected to protect her heart and soul. He had found the key to unlock all of her. Why did the one man who had accomplished that have to be the one man who wasn't in a position to return her feelings? The one whose life and work were somewhere else.

Still, the single promise she had kept to herself after life with Mark was that she wanted to live in the moment. The feelings she felt, all the butterflies and fire mixed into one, had to be expressed in some manner. So, Sandra gave herself into the moment as Trey bent to kiss her.

"I shouldn't do this." His breath feathered her lips, making them numb with anticipation.

Their lips touched and he played with hers with a light brush. He was tentative at first and then a hunger deep within seemed to possess both of them. Gathering her closer, they explored each other in depth.

She consciously made note of every little aspect of their kiss and his touch so she could bring this moment back to life as she fell asleep every night. She memorized his touch as he slid his hands down to her backside, pulling her even closer. There was no denying his physical response to her. He was hard and wanting her and she groaned at both the contact and the power she had over him.

Breaking their kiss, he headed south of her mouth and she tilted her neck so he had easy access. Goosebumps broke out on her arms and she became breathless with the need for him. When he took a finger and traced ever so softly along the "v" of her neckline and followed that with his lips, her knees would have given out if he hadn't had her pinned up against the wall.

She was breathing hard, as was he. Trey kissed the pulse at the base of her neck before returning to her lips. She eagerly accepted his mouth. He covered her gasp as he cupped her breast and used his thumb to bring her nipple to aching life. The world and noise faded away and she was completely lost in the moment.

When he broke the kiss again, he didn't move to her neck as before, causing her to open her eyes. His eyes were glazed, reflecting, she was sure, what her eyes spoke volumes of.

He reached into his shirt pocket for something. The movement confused her initially. She was ready for round two of their make-out session. Disappointment washed through her as she realized he was answering his phone. That at least explained the buzzing she had been feeling against her chest.

"Walker." He didn't take his eyes off her as he answered. Somehow he had managed to control his breathing. "When?" She didn't like the change of expression that crossed his face as he continued to ask one-word questions. "Where?"

When he hung up, he let out a sigh. He leaned his forehead against hers. His silence and the music in the background tempered her racing heart and slowed her breathing to a less erratic pace. She knew what the call was about and her heart hurt.

"They've caught him."

She could only nod, the lump in her throat preventing her from speaking. Mark being caught was a good thing and he couldn't hurt her now. His threats were once again just that, threats. The news should have made her feel relief. Her life could go back to normal. Her house would be her home again. No more running into the two men who had invaded her space the past several days.

But all she felt was a sense of loss.

Although the space they were in was small, she became chilled when Trey's warm body pulled back.

"Umm...they've already lined me up with another job which starts first thing in the morning, so I have to leave tonight." He ran his hand through his hair, a sure sign he wasn't happy about something.

Sandra swallowed hard so the lump in her throat would disappear.

"Well, I..." She managed a smile, but not one that reached her eyes. "I... thank you."

That was lame, but she couldn't think of anything to say. Her heart had shattered at the news.

"I need to find Logan. He's not going to be thrilled to leave Lacy behind."

She shrugged. "They'll figure something out if it's worth working on."

Would he respond to this? Would he think that maybe they could work on a relationship?

"I guess."

He brushed her face as he tucked a strand of hair behind her ear. His hand lingered. He cupped her face and offered a final kiss. She hungrily accepted. With one final brush of her lips, he captured her hand and led her out of their hiding spot. She stood behind him while he scanned the room for Danny.

They found him talking with Lacy and Sandra's mom. Sandra managed a smile as they came upon the group and immediately felt lost when Trey dropped her hand right before they joined them.

He let them finish the conversation they were in the middle of before taking Danny aside. With her arms crossed, she half listened to Lacy and Donna talk. She was aware when Maggie joined them, but her attention was on the guys as Trey told Danny the news. Danny glanced at Lacy briefly as the message was relayed to him and then back to Trey, nodding when he was done talking.

They walked back to the group. While Danny took Lacy to one side, Trey announced the good news to the rest of the group.

"You'll be glad to know they've captured Mark Franklin. Your daughter's life is no longer in danger, Donna. This also means Logan and I are off of the case as of now, and because of a new responsibility tomorrow, we need to leave tonight."

Donna clasped her hands together before giving Sandra a big hug. This time Sandra couldn't keep the tears from her eyes. She hoped Trey would believe that the relief of the capture and her Mom's emotions were what triggered them and not her heart was breaking into tiny pieces. Foolish she knew. A foolish woman who had let her emotions overrule her logic.

As he had hoped, Mark had no problem fitting into the crowd as another local. The large number of people was both good fortune and a curse. The crowd gave him a chance to keep from standing out, but they also made it difficult to keep an eye on Sandra.

He first spotted her at the bar where the bartender flirted with her and then the big guy took her onto the dance floor. He lost them after that for several minutes and was starting to wonder if they had left.

Mark finally spotted them again in a group with the big guy's sidekick, the hot blond from the gym and two older women. It wasn't until the two guys stepped to one side that he recognized Sandra's mother. He hadn't seen her since the day his verdict was read. She had clapped at the guilty verdict and had had the audacity to stare him down when he left the courtroom.

He returned his gaze to Sandra who was standing quietly. The gentlemen returned to the group. The lanky one pulled the hot blond to one side. Something was going on.

A petite redhead slowly passed by him making eye contact and smiling. He returned the smile and touched his fingers to the brim of his hat. She walked on by glancing once over her shoulder while he appreciated the sway of her hips, his groin responding to the obvious invitation. If he had more time, he would have charmed her out of her cowboy boots.

Mark dragged his eyes from the object of his lust and discovered Sandra was no longer on the floor. He cursed but then sighed with relief when he saw them by the bar. The bartender was at it again, hitting on Sandra, but there was something different. The two guys were no longer with her.

Mark took the time to scan the immediate area, but still didn't see either one of them. He frowned and wondered where they had gone. Taking a chance the women would be at the bar for a few more seconds, he scanned the rest of the room. He wondered for a minute if they had seen him and were surrounding him, but there was nothing. They couldn't be found.

His gaze returned to the ladies as Donna was asked to dance. Another woman approached the group as Donna took to the dance floor. He didn't recognize her, but he appreciated that she had a lot going on for an older woman. He had gone far too long without a woman as once again his groin responded. He looked forward to meeting up with Megan in Mexico and ending his dry spell.

Relaxing a little, he leaned against the wall and kept his eye on the women as they were each asked to dance. He would know when the moment was right. The redhead continued vying for his attention, but he ignored her, intent on one thing. Accomplishing his mission.

———

"TREY SEEMS like a nice guy once you get past his brusqueness."

Sandra glanced at her mom. "That was business."

"Mm."

"What is that suppose to mean?"

"Just, mm? Nothing more?"

"Mom, you don't know the meaning of nothing more, so if there is something you want to say, say it."

Donna turned toward her, smiling, as Sandra guarded herself against the emotions swirling like a hurricane in her stomach.

"I'm just saying he was nice."

"And?"

"And I think you agree and aren't willing to admit it."

"I guess he was nice enough."

Donna touched her daughter's arm. "Honey, you may have yourself fooled, but you can't fool your mom. With what little time I've spent with you these last few days it is obvious there was something between the two of you."

Sandra couldn't say anything and instead watched the dancers. Maggie and Lacy were both on the floor smiling and enjoying their time. Danny and Lacy had already made plans to see each other in a few weeks.

How do you admit to your mother that a guy you have only known for a few days has penetrated the heart you have hardened? Sandra tried to convince herself that the lonely years were why this whole emotional mess had come about, but she knew that was a lie.

"There was nothing between the two of us. He was here to do a job. It's as simple as that."

"That's not what I saw."

Sandra faced her mother. "What do you want me to say? Trey is an attractive male specimen. It would be hard not to notice. That's his good quality. Let me list the not so attractive parts. He's stubborn, has an ego the size of New York, is opinionated, and he doesn't listen to reason." For emphasis, Sandra counted off each of his faults using her fingers.

Smiling, Donna watched as dancers dispersed from the

dance floor while others merged onto the floor. "Sounds like love to me."

"Mom, you have to jump off that train of thought." Sandra was frustrated. Having her mother voice what she was fully aware of, frightened her.

Trey was gone and he wasn't coming back. He had shaken hands with her. Shaken hands. No smile, just a simple goodbye and good luck. When they had left she watched as Danny glanced over his shoulder blowing Lacy a kiss. But Trey? He had kept walking.

She was saved from any more questions from her mother when a gentleman came and asked Donna to dance. Sandra was still feeling the buzz from the shots she had had early in the evening. She sipped on a Coke while she watched the dancers. The band was great, the drinks were flowing, and everyone seemed to be having the best time. Except for her.

Well, why not her?

Sandra straightened her shoulders and looked around the floor to see if there was anyone she could ask to dance. As her glance slid along the perimeter of the crowd and the walls, something caught her eye. She thought there had been a man standing there who had seemed familiar, yet out of place. He was gone now. She shrugged. It must have been her imagination.

"May I have this dance?"

She smiled at Billy. "I would love to."

"Come on Logan, I'm ready to go. What's taking you so long?"

"Almost done, Boss. Just have to grab my toothbrush."

Trey glanced at his watch. They had only been gone from the dance for forty minutes and he was still concerned about Sandra. He kept reminding himself she was safe. They had Franklin and he couldn't hurt her.

So why did he have this feeling something wasn't right? Was

it because the assignment seemed to have ended so abruptly? In the past, notification of a capture had come in steps. They usually knew of the impending arrest and then the final capture. To be notified immediately of the capture had thrown him off, he decided. He had to process this one differently.

"Okay, I'm ready."

Trey tossed Logan the SUV keys. "You drive ours and I'll take Sandra's car so we can drop it off at the dance."

They threw their bags into the SUV and Trey climbed into Sandra's car. He had to adjust the seat to accommodate his long legs while trying to ignore her smell, which lingered, trapped in the interior of the car. Starting the engine, he put the car in reverse and followed Logan down the street.

The trip back to the community center gave him too much time to think. Saying goodbye to her had been tough. He could read her like a book. She had stared at him, confusion clouding her eyes, when he had simply shaken her hand.

What she didn't know is that if he had taken her in his arms again, he would have picked her up, carried her away and taken her back to her place to make slow love to her. But he hadn't had the luxury for that when another job waited for him the next afternoon. So he had turned into the hard-assed Marshal she had met on the first day and had hated that. He wouldn't have a chance to get in touch with her until after this next assignment. He hit the steering wheel out of frustration.

That had been too close. When Sandra had started scanning the room he thought she had recognized him. Mark had turned his back and quickly hid behind three people engaged in conversation. He managed to weave his way to the back of the building by sticking to the wall and going from group to group. Settling down closer to the back of the building still gave him good access to watch the dance floor as well as the front of the building.

Once settled, he saw Sandra on the dance floor with the young bartender and watched as he held her tight for the slow dance and rubbed his hand up and down her back. A sneer crossed Mark's face.

Enjoy it now, buddy, 'cause after tonight you will never have the opportunity again.

A movement caught his eye and he watched as Donna headed to the back of the community center where he knew the bathrooms were located. She stood out in the bright pink top and was easy to keep an eye on as she made her way through the throngs of people. He started after her, a plan forming on how to separate Sandra from the crowd.

Mark waited until he was sure Donna had entered the ladies' room before moving down the hallway after her. There wasn't anyone else in sight and he hoped it stayed that way. The women's bathroom was the last one on the right near the back exit. Positioning himself between the exit and the bathroom door, he waited.

———

"BILLY, please keep your hands above my waist."

"Come on, babe, we've been playing this cat-and-mouse game far too long."

Nuzzling her neck and once again sliding his hands where they didn't belong, he whispered, "You know you want this as bad as I do."

She pushed away from him and put her hands on her hips. "I don't care to be pawed by an awkward boy. Let me know when you are ready to act like a gentleman and then we can talk."

She returned to the table where she had left her Coke and now was wishing there was liquor in her cup. Billy had picked the wrong night to try to worm his way into her life. She had gone from sad to pissed in a short period of time and had taken her anger over Trey out on Billy. The burst of anger cleared her head for the moment. She watched the others dance.

Her mother had been dancing with a variety of men and was enjoying herself, smiling and chatting them up. She watched her mom disengage herself from the next dance and head to the rear of the building. Must be time for a potty break.

Several minutes passed while Sandra watched Maggie, Lacy and Wendy dance. She realized she was a little mesmerized, watching Wendy rub her body against her dance partners during the slow dance. That seemed a little desperate, but Wendy seemed bound and determined not to go home alone. The encounter with Trey leading her to believe he was gay seemed to have put her on track to find a heterosexual. Sandra chuckled.

"Well, honey, I'm sure glad to see you have found your sense of humor again."

Sandra turned to find Frank at her elbow. He kissed her on the cheek and joined her at the table. "I've never lost my sense of humor."

"Really? I could have sworn it left with that tall dark and please-take-me-home Marshal dude."

"Did my mom send you over here?"

"Fat chance. I don't need anyone's mother to send me on errands."

"Well, do me a favor. Stay away from her then. I don't need you two to start comparing notes." Sandra gave Frank a loving smile.

"Are you Sandra?"

Chapter 18

Sandra found a pretty, petite redhead standing next to her. "Yes I am. Why?"

"Your mother isn't feeling well and wants you to take her home."

"Oh." She looked around the room thinking her mom was somewhere there, but didn't see her. "Where is she?"

"She went out the exit by the bathrooms for some fresh air."

"Thank you. Sorry Frank. If I'm not back tonight I'll call you tomorrow."

"Do you want me to go with you?"

"Oh, no. Thanks, I'll be fine."

Sandra wove her way through the crowd, excusing herself as she made her way to the back of the grange. There were a few people in the hallway to the bathroom she had to navigate through before she reached the exit. Sandra hurried out the door, glancing to her left and then her right. She saw her mom crumpled on the cold, hard ground.

"Mom!" Sandra rushed to her side crouching down and checking for a pulse, relieved to find one. "Mom.... Mom...wake up." She shook her a little, hoping the movement would help.

"She'll wake up, but it'll be awhile."

That voice. The hair rose on Sandra's arms and she thought she was going to throw up. She slowly stood and turned to face the man who had given her nightmares. His image shocked her. He was thinner than she remembered. His face was covered with a scruffy beard and he had the brim of his hat pulled down low. No designer clothes for him now. He was as nondescript as the next person.

The last time she had seen him, he was dressed impeccably in a dark gray, custom-made Italian suit with a white shirt and light gray tie. That was the night she had confronted him about his embezzling. That was always how she saw him in her nightmares.

The man standing in front of her was still full of ego and self-righteousness. When you are in love with someone, you overlook his or her weaknesses. Apparently, love truly was blind. She had overlooked the kind of person Mark was and had placed him in the category she thought he should be in. The signs had been there, she had simply ignored them.

"What did you do to her?" Sandra squatted next to her mother again, rechecking Donna's pulse, relieved that there was a steady beat. She smoothed the hair off Donna's face and ran her hands over her head, discovering a lump. She wished she had a pillow to put under her head.

"Nothing that will kill her. Yet."

"Mom? Mom, can you hear me?" She rubbed her mom's face again, hoping to see her eyes flutter open.

Sandra took some slow breaths to calm her racing heart. She didn't want Mark to know she was scared. She needed to dig deep to find the strength to survive this.

"Okay, so you found me." Maybe if she kept him talking long enough, someone would find them. "Now what?"

"Now you and I go on a road trip."

"And if I refuse?"

He glanced at her mom and back at her. "It'd be awful to have your Dad lose two people."

Anger rose in her, temporarily replacing the fear. "My mom has nothing to do with us."

"That's totally up to you."

The music coming from the center was muffled. Crickets were chirping in the cool spring night, with a few frogs chiming in for a little harmony. At any other time Sandra would have enjoyed the outdoor symphony. Instead she was trying desperately to figure out how to keep Mark talking long enough for someone to discover them.

"Come on, Sandra, stop wasting time. You and I have a date with destiny."

She heard a click and snapped her head back to him. He was backlit from the light by the door and crouched as she was she couldn't see his face. His body language said it all, though. As if he didn't have a care in the world, he held a gun in his right hand and it was pointed directly at her. Sandra stood slowly and the gun followed her.

"Mark, think about this. Think about your parents and sister. This isn't what they would want you to do."

"It doesn't matter what they want, it's what I want. You screwed me over. We were engaged and you turned on me. You have no sense of loyalty."

"You stole from your clients."

"I got what was owed me."

"Including time."

The muscles around his jaw tightened and Sandra realized she might have pushed him too far. The sound of a car distracted them. They turned towards the noise as headlights swept the back of the parking lot. Relief and hope surged through her, but it was short-lived as Mark wrapped his arm around her neck and covering her mouth to keep her from screaming.

"Don't say one word or make a sound. If you do, I can guarantee Donna will meet you at the pearly gates. Do you understand?" Sandra nodded and he released her. "Come on."

Glancing back at her mother, Sandra stumbled along beside Mark as he hurried her across the uneven ground, away from the community center. Pain shot through her arm as his fingers dug into her.

She had to do something. If Mark took her off the property, she was dead for sure. Now that they were away from her Mom, she had to think clearly what her next step should be.

At the entrance of the center, Logan parked the car while Trey drove past to find a parking spot for Sandra's car. The spot they had vacated was no longer there which forced Trey to head out into the marked-off area of the field. He found an empty spot just a few rows in.

His mood hadn't improved any on the drive. Something wasn't right but he couldn't put his finger on it. He kept running the conversation he had had with his boss, Shelly, through his mind. Maybe he needed to call her and have some questions answered. He would do that after he gave Sandra her keys.

His phone rang as he opened the car door. It was his boss. Slamming the door, he answered the phone as he locked the car.

"Hey, Shelly."

"Walker, we have a problem."

"A problem?" Trey headed to the front of the building.

"We don't have Franklin after all. It was some guy in a stolen car that fit his description."

"What the hell, Shelly!" He took off running, motioning for Logan to follow him. Logan jumped out of the SUV and caught up with Trey in seconds.

"He's still out there, Walker. We received a phone call tonight from a guy who owns a doughnut shop there in Ferry City. He says a guy matching Franklin's description exactly was in his shop both yesterday and today."

"And he's just now calling."

"He didn't see the news until tonight."

Trey didn't answer. He had already hung up.

"Logan, it wasn't Franklin they caught. We need to find Sandra quickly."

They stood at the entrance to the community center, searching the dance floor and the people lining the walls.

Trey didn't like the feel of this. Sandra wasn't anywhere to be found. Her friends and Maggie were near the bar laughing and talking. He took a step towards them when a gunshot rang out. Then a second one.

Both Marshals drew their guns and were through the double doors before the second shot had stopped echoing. Trey led the way, sticking to the shadows of the wall and going as fast as he dared. Logan was right behind him.

He needed to assess where the shots had come from. As he neared the back of the building, he slowed and came to a stop before reaching the light that would have given him away. With his back against the wall and the gun in both hands, he leaned over to scan the lit area at the back door.

Shit!

He turned to Logan motioning him to be silent. They listened, waiting to hear where the man with the gun was. Trey had no doubt it was Franklin.

Had he shot Sandra? Was she bleeding to death in the dark?

Sweat broke out on his forehead. Then he heard him. It wasn't very loud, but the night carried his voice.

"Come on, Sandra. Make it easy on yourself. You don't really want me to go back and shoot Donna, do you?"

As if he found his comment humorous, he laughed softly.

Trey turned to Logan motioning for him to stay put while he worked his way around the cars, closing the distance between him and Franklin. Before slipping into the night, Trey showed Logan the motionless body of Donna by the back entrance.

"Watch her," he barely breathed to Logan and received a nod in return.

Trey stepped back a few feet, keeping out of the light as he slipped into the night, using the cars for cover. As he had hoped, Franklin continued to give his location away.

———

SANDRA KNEW, as she stumbled through the dark with Mark, that she was going to have to take action soon. She needed to stay where there were people.

"Ow!" She stumbled to the ground, jerking her arm out of Mark's grasp and scraping her knees in the process. She used the cover of darkness to find a rock.

"Get up, you bitch."

"My ankle."

"Like I give a damn." Mark grabbed her arm again, pulling hard. Pain shot through her shoulder as he half-lifted her off the ground.

"Okay, okay, just a second."

She stood slowly, buying time. His hand was wrapped tight around her arm. As she lifted her shoulders and head, she used the momentum to swing her other hand with the rock directly at his head. By the time, he realized what was happening, she had already made contact. Mark dropped her arm and Sandra took off into the dark, diving for the cover of the nearest car as a shot rang out. Mark shot at her again and she heard the bullet hit the dirt behind her.

Scrambling to her feet, Sandra took off as quietly as she

could in a crouched position, working her way from car to car, far away from Mark, she hoped. Sandra stopped to catch her breath. Her heart was racing and it was hard to breathe quietly. She had to suppress the urge to gulp for air.

"Sandra. Honey. It's no use running. It won't bother me if there are witnesses."

Damn. She had thought she had put more distance between them. Mark's voice carried from only a few cars away and dripped with sarcasm. His voice wasn't loud, but it carried through the stillness of the night air.

Chills raced down her spine. Would he hurt anyone who came between him and her? She heard the crunch of gravel as he started walking again, toward her.

She forced down the sob that was threatening to give her away and crept slowly around the car she was using as a shield. Each step was slow and deliberate so the sound of gravel didn't give her away.

Clutching the edge of the passenger's side window, Sandra slowly raised her head to peer through the glass, ducking when she saw Mark on the driver's side, his back to her. She squatted where she was, barely breathing, waiting for his next move.

"Come on, baby. You know it's inevitable. It doesn't make any difference that it's dark. I'll find you." He chuckled. "I promise."

His voice made her to flinch. She pushed down the panic that was threatening to override her common sense to stay put. Her muscles were screaming from staying crouched. How she wished Trey Walker were here.

The sound of gravel alerted her that Mark was moving. She held her breath, letting it out slowly as the sound grew fainter. He was moving away from her. Leg muscles protesting, she eased her way up to once again peer through the car windows. She watched him walk between the cars making his way towards the front of the community center.

"Come out, come out, wherever you are."

She could hear the smile in his voice. Not for the first time, she wondered what she had found attractive about this man. Besides mistaking his ego for confidence, that is.

To ease her muscles, Sandra straightened her legs, staying bent at the waist and reaching for her feet. The stretch brought immediate relief.

Okay, now what.

She needed help. Mark was heading around to the front, so she headed for the back entrance. She would worry about the light exposure once she was closer.

Where was Trey? Had the phone call been part of Mark's plan? Oh, God, she thought, please bring Trey Walker back.

Mark's next words chilled her. "Perhaps I need to go take of Donna."

Her mom. She was still hurt and Mark had to only walk back over and put a bullet in her.

"You wouldn't get any satisfaction from it." She didn't question why she had spoken. She had to draw his attention away from her mom. He wanted her too badly.

Sandra moved quickly after making her location known. A shot rang out, shattering the window of a car near where she had been. Mark had used three bullets, which meant he had three left in the chamber. This was a dangerous game of Marco Polo, but she had to keep him believing he could catch her. To keep him from returning to her mom.

There had to be someone who had heard the shots.

Any minute now she would hear sirens. She had to. Panic threatened to paralyze her, but she had to stay calm in order to survive. In order to save her mom.

Sandra continued to dodge through the cars.

"Come on, baby. Why are you making this difficult?"

He was like a heat-seeking missile. He seemed to sense the

direction she was headed. She wanted to scream as another shot rang out, but he was too close.

A hand suddenly clamped over her mouth. An arm encircled her ribs, crushing her against a solid chest. She grabbed at the hand, trying to pull it away from her mouth.

Oh, God .how had he found her?

Sandra finally recognized the whispered reassurances near her ear. Her other senses registered the familiarity of the chest she was pressed against. Relief flooded her veins.

Oh, God, *Trey had found her.*

He removed his hand and she turned. Staring back at her were the eyes of the man she thought she would never see again.

———

TREY GRABBED SANDRA'S HAND, motioning for her to follow him. Crouched and on tiptoes, they made their way quietly and slowly away from Franklin.

"If you aren't going to make this easy, then I guess your mom is first." Mark's laugh was low. "I found you once, so have no doubt I'll find you again."

They heard him walking, but not back to Donna. His steps were slow and deliberate. It was as Trey had figured. Franklin had one mission in mind and that was Sandra. He motioned for her to stay put.

Because Franklin thought that only Sandra and he were in the parking lot, he hadn't bothered to hide. The partial moonlight allowed Trey to make Franklin out as he walked among the cars. Franklin kept walking slowly towards the front of the building. Every few steps he stopped to listen and taunt Sandra. Each time he moved, Trey moved.

Trey's movements were quick and quiet. He had years of tracking experience on his side while Franklin was driven by revenge. The need was great making Franklin careless, now that his target was close. Trey knew the thought of being captured was no longer on Franklin's radar.

Trey became aware of voices at the front of the building. Franklin did too. A quick glance confirmed that a group of at least five people was heading out to the parking lot. The parking lot where they were playing cat-and-mouse. Trey swore under his breath.

"Oh, don't worry, Sandra, I see I have some target practices coming to join us. Is this really how you want the night to end? Innocent people getting hurt over what's between you and I?"

Trey took advantage of Franklin mouthing off to creep closer. He wanted to make sure his shot was perfect if Franklin raised his gun.

"What the hell!"

Trey froze. Had Franklin seen him? Had he heard him? He glanced at Franklin and followed his gaze over to where the group had been seconds ago. There was nothing. No voices, no sound of steps in the gravel. Had they sensed the danger and hidden?

Unfortunately, the moment was short-lived as a couple rounded the corner from the front, giggling and talking. Franklin turned his attention on them.

"This is even better, Sandra. I have a bullet for each of them with one left in the chamber for you."

"Hey, Franklin. Why don't you pick on someone your own size?"

Even Trey was startled for a second as he saw Logan, gun drawn, step out of the building's shadow where the group had disappeared. Two things registered. Logan must have pulled the group out of harm's way and it was now or never to take down Franklin.

In the light of the moon, Trey watched Franklin break into a grin and refocus his gun on Logan. "Well, well, if we don't have the scrawny bodyguard showing off his muscles."

"I'd think twice about it, Franklin." Trey was within fifteen feet and held his gun in both hands pointed at Franklin's head. "U.S. Marshal. You're under arrest."

Franklin turned slowly to his left until his gun, still in position to shoot, was now pointed at Trey.

"Drop the gun, Franklin. It's over. You have two guns aimed at you. The odds are stacked against you."

More people were spilling from the community center as it became obvious the dance had come to an end. Distant sirens pierced the night and Franklin was starting to waver.

———

SANDRA HEARD Trey tell Mark to put his gun down and made her way toward her mom, remaining crouched behind the cars.

She left the safety of the last car and ran to her mom. As she stepped into the light of the back entrance, she was relieved to see her mom stirring.

"Mom?"

The sound was loud as if it had been amplified. The sharp noise echoed into the night followed simultaneously by another loud sound.

"Sandra!" Her mother's scream seemed distant.

The shots registered in the recess of Sandra's mind, but not the physical impact of the bullet. She stumbled as she continued toward her mother. She had a pressing need to protect her mom, but Sandra's vision was becoming blurred and her mind hazy.

Sandra fell to her knees. She became aware of the burning in her right shoulder and felt something wet trickling down her back before blackness overtook her.

Chapter 19

Everything hurt. Even her hair hurt. She felt as if she was coming out of a dark tunnel. There was something humming. What was humming in her bedroom? Where was Tiny? He should be taken out. Why couldn't she open her eyes? They were too heavy to open.

"Her hand moved. Sandra, can you hear me?"

What was her mom doing in her bedroom? Why did she sound close to tears?

She felt her mom's hand brush at her forehead and felt her hand squeezed. "Honey, open your eyes."

It's too hard, Mom. I'm too tired.

Her mom's voice faded and Sandra fell back into a deep sleep.

The rustling of papers registered through Sandra's foggy mind immediately followed by a dull pain. Her lids didn't feel as weighted but were slow to open. The lights were low and she glanced around the room, confused as to why her head seemed heavy.

This wasn't her bedroom. A woman in nurses clothing was standing at the sink, reading papers.

Sandra's mouth opened but nothing came out. Her mouth was parched. She noticed ice chips on the table next to her, but her right arm was strapped to her body. A groan escaped as she tried to move.

"Hey there, Sandra." The nurse moved to her bedside, taking her left wrist between her fingers to check her pulse. "My name is Mindy. I'm your nurse for the next few hours."

Sandra tried to speak again, but only a raspy noise escaped. Mindy released her wrist and turned back to write the numbers in her chart. She tucked the pen behind her ear before returning her attention to Sandra.

"Let me take your temperature and then I'll give you some ice chips." She swiped an instrument across her forehead. "Good. It's normal."

As she promised, Mindy scooped a few chips onto a spoon and fed them to Sandra. She had never tasted anything so good and closed her eyes to savor the hard coolness as it melted in her mouth. Her mouth automatically opened for more as the last of the ice dissolved. After several scoops, she finally felt she could function.

Still a little raspy, she managed to utter a few words. "Why am I here?"

"You were shot in the right shoulder and spent a few hours in surgery. You're probably still feeling effects of the anesthesia as well as the pain killers."

Sandra digested the information, but her brain was still fuzzy and slow. Images raced through her mind until the puzzle pieces started falling into place.

"My mom. Was my mom hurt?"

Mindy patted her arm with reassurance. "Your mom is fine. She has a nasty bump on her head with a slight concussion, but is doing great. She spent the night for observation and should be released today. She was very worried about you and spent an hour with you until we shooed her off to her room."

Sandra closed her eyes, the exertion of the conversation tiring her.

"Is there anything else you need?"

She opened her eyes. "If you could sit me up a little, I'm sure I can do the chips myself."

Mindy adjusted her, finished her chart work and left promising to check on her in an hour. Sandra slept.

"Honey, it's Mom."

Sandra's eyes opened more willingly than the last time she had attempted. Her mom looked wonderful and tears sprung to Sandra's eyes. She blinked quickly to rid them before they could fall.

"Oh, Mom. Are you okay?"

"I still have a headache, but otherwise am fine. I've been so worried about you."

"Hi, Sandra."

Maggie stood at the bottom of her bed. "Hi, Maggie." She returned her attention to Donna. "Tell me everything that happened last night? I remember racing to you and then must have blacked out after being shot."

"I thought he had killed you." Donna choked up a little, tears springing to her eyes. "I thought I had lost you," she whispered.

Sandra grabbed Donna's hand. "You didn't." She chuckled a little to break the seriousness of the situation. "I must have nine lives."

Donna smiled and wiped her eyes. "It's the good Irish stock. Thank your father for that. He should be here shortly, by the way. That wasn't exactly the kind of phone call he wanted in the middle of the night."

"Go on with the story."

"There's not much more to tell. You were shot and both

Danny and Trey shot Mark." Donna took Sandra's hand in both of hers. "He can't bother you any more."

A twinge of sadness for Mark's family touched Sandra for a brief moment. Their son and brother's promising career had turned into a media circus three years ago and now they had to go through the tragedy of his death.

"And Danny and Walker?" She tried to ask the question casually. "Are they both okay?"

"They're fine. I'm sure they would have been here, but they had to complete their reports to the Agency. Because of the shooting, they were both put on paid leave for a while."

A knock at the door interrupted them. Lacy was hesitant to walk in. "Can I come in?"

"Oh, Lacy, yes."

She carried in a bouquet of pink roses. "I wanted you to have a little color in this drab place."

"They're beautiful. Thank you."

"Everyone is going nuts wanting to know how you are. My phone has been ringing off the hook." She gave a wave of her hand. "And the rumor mill has outdone itself. Everything from a jilted lover to the mafia has crept into stories."

The rest of the afternoon consisted of catnaps and a parade of her friends. Sandra attempted to make light of her past, but her friends manage to dig every detail out of her. When Frank came by, his first question was about Trey.

"You do understand, Frank, he's not gay."

"Well, I was willing to change his mind if he'd given me half a chance." Frank winked. "Here's the story I've heard thus far. You were the head of a mafia family and Mark Franklin double-crossed you. You sent him to jail, quit the mafia to start over here, are having a love child with Walker, and also won the lottery."

"Wow. Who knew I was so busy."

The comment made for a good laugh and Sandra once again explained her past.

Sleep was hard to come by that night between the interruptions of the nurses and the nightmares of Mark pointing a gun at her. Near morning exhaustion won out and Sandra fell into a deep slumber void of dreams.

———

IT HAD BEEN two weeks since the shooting and Sandra was sitting in her office sorting through the mail with her left hand. On Monday, she planned to re-open her fitness center, which had been closed since the shooting. Until her arm healed there weren't going to be any massages, but, on the upside, her personal training had picked up. Who knew a good shoot 'em up story would do wonders for her business.

She had contacted Mark's parents, but they made it clear they didn't want her sympathy. As Mark had done, his parents blamed her for the family's disgrace.

The one person she had been hoping to hear from, she hadn't. Lacy had been in contact with Danny every day since he had left. They had met up over the weekend as well. But Sandra hadn't heard from Trey. Even Tiny seemed to be a little down over how quiet the house was once again.

Lost in her thoughts, she failed to hear the front door open. A movement caught her eye and for a moment she thought maybe she had hallucinated Trey leaning against her doorjamb.

He appeared relaxed. His hands were tucked into the front pockets of his faded jeans, the tail of his shirt scrunched under his thumbs. His chin was covered in a scruff of whiskers that managed to make him appear sexier, if that was possible. How could a man look so delicious?

"Hey."

His voice fanned the flames in the pit of her stomach. The warmth ran rapidly to the end of her toes and fingers and she found herself feeling a bit light headed from the rush.

"Hey? You don't say goodbye and I haven't seen you in two weeks and that's it?"

Sandra leaned back in her chair, trying to act nonchalant, knowing full well the pulse at the base of her neck contradicted her attempt.

"No reason to ask how you're doing. You must be doing well enough since you're at work."

"I am."

"I stopped by to let you know you were right."

"Can I get that in writing?" Her question extracted a chuckle from him.

"That could be arranged."

That smile. She couldn't get enough of that smile. "And what was I right about?"

Trey pushed off from the doorframe and walked over to the desk. But rather than stop as she had expected and plop into the chair in front of her, he walked around to where she sat.

"We need to talk."

"Okay?" She turned her chair a fraction and looked up at him. "What do you want to talk about?"

Sandra cautioned her heart. She didn't want to get her hopes up. Not only had he not said goodbye and had ignored her since the shooting, but he hadn't checked to see how she was healing. He may simply be here to say goodbye now. Perhaps this was his way of putting closure to a case.

She felt a bit of anger at herself for being foolish in believing Trey was here for anything more than saying goodbye and good luck.

He suddenly turned her towards him and placed both hands on the arms of her chair causing her look directly into his eyes.

As quick as the anger appeared it dissipated. She was back to feeling light headed as she noted something different in his eyes.

"You were right. I need to relax more. I need a relationship with someone who is my equal and wants to be a partner in all things."

Sandra swallowed. Hard. Was he referring to her or was there another woman he had in mind.

"I want to make Ferry City my home base. And I want to take on this crazy ass world with you."

Sandra could now let the joy that had been slowly rising as he spoke to burst through. "I think that can be arranged."

She smiled at him as he leaned in and kissed her. Sandra wondered as she grabbed the back of his neck with her left hand, if feeling his lips on hers would ever get old. She didn't think so.

ACKNOWLEDGMENTS

Thank you, thank you for all the support I have received from so many of my family and friends. A special thanks to my editor Holly Doering as well as my number one beta reader and good friend, Cindi Bughi. You two rock! The cover art is from the fabulous Lee Hyat. Thank you Lee for your patience with a newbie. Thank you to my "Moms" group (Gay, Heidi, Gaylene, Theresa and Joanne) for your input and support. To my kids, who write so much better than me, Bryce, Brianna and Patrick for pushing me forward. And a special thanks to my number one fan, my husband, Roger. Even though you have yet to read anything I've written, your support has been unconditional.

ABOUT THE AUTHOR

Teresa Woodworth lives outside of Spokane, WA with her husband of 35 years. They have three grown kids and three absolutely adorable grandkids. She got her love of story telling from her dad. He was definitely the king of story telling.
Contact Teresa at teresawoodworth@comcast.net.
Follow her on Twitter @teresawoodworth as well as Instagram.

 twitter.com/teresawoodworth

 instagram.com/teresawoodworth